0(

THE FANTASTIC BICYCLES BOOK

Steven Lindblom

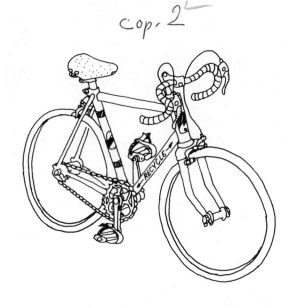

Houghton Mifflin Company Boston 1979

To True

Library of Congress Cataloging in Publication Data

Lindblom, Steven.
  The fantastic bicycles book.

  SUMMARY: Discusses recycling bicycles, including
where to find cheap and free bikes and parts, how to
make repairs, and how to combine parts to make projects
such as three-wheelers and tandems.
    1. Bicycles and tricycles – Design and construction
– Juvenile literature. [1. Bicycles and bicycling]
I. Title.
TL410.L48   629.22'72   79-15281
ISBN 0-395-28481-3
ISBN 0-395-28482-1 pbk.

Contents

Making Bikes Better

Odds and Ends

Introduction

This book is about bicycles, but it is especially about thrown-out bikes that you get for nothing—where to find them, how to fix them up, and things you can make with bike parts, like three-wheelers, dirt bikes or tandems.

The bike is as perfect a machine as there is, and parts from one made in America will fit another made in India. Cared for, a bike will last forever. Anyone can fix it. Parts are cheap. All of which makes it an ideal machine to recycle. In most parts of the world a bicycle never wears out but is repaired and, if beyond repair, broken up for parts to fix other bikes.

But here in the U.S.A. millions get junked every year, often for no more reason than a flat tire, dry bearing, or just because the kids have grown up! This, of course, is a horrible waste. But it also means that there are a lot of bikes and parts out there for free if you're willing to do a little work.

Scavenging and Recycling

Scavenging, as it applies to this book, is the art of finding what you need to build something without spending much money. Why bother when you can just buy everything new and avoid all the running around? For one thing, if you haven't spent a lot of money on a project you don't have to take it too seriously. If you don't finish it, you don't have to feel guilty. If you do finish it and decide you don't like it, all you've lost is time, and if you just plain enjoy building things, not even that.

But there's another even better reason for recycling. Everything we use is made of raw materials that are produced using energy. In the case of a bike the materials are steel, a bit of rubber, chrome, and paint, along with the coal and electricity that run the steel mill and factory, and the labor of the workers who put it all together. These materials, once used, have been invested, and the return on the investment is the use to be had from the bike. When a bike is junked after a few years the investment is wiped out. A new bike is built to replace the junked one, using up more materials, energy, and labor. But if you find that junk bike and fix it up, then that's one less new bicycle that'll be needed. And you've got a bike for free! Not because it necessarily cost you nothing, but because it didn't cost the earth anymore of its precious and dwindling resources.

Finding Junk Bicycles

Old bikes are not hard to find unless you're in a hurry, in which case you'll probably end up looking in a bike store. There, the used bikes will be selling for thirty dollars and up. Don't pay it. Be patient, keep your eyes open and something will turn up for a few dollars or less. This goes doubly if you already have a bike for everyday riding and want another to fool around with. No use chopping up a good bike someone else could be riding to make yourself an exercise bike!

Good places to find a cheap bike, or parts to make one, are town dumps (sometimes the dump attendant saves and sells them, usually cheap), yard sales, police auctions (most police departments auction off the unclaimed lost-and-found bicycles once or twice a year. Beware, though, there is something about the excitement of an auction that can get prices up higher than the things are worth), junk and secondhand stores, and Goodwill or Salvation Army shops. Or check out college dorm or fraternity house trash piles in June when students move out. Someone in your neighborhood whose kids have grown up might have a bike collecting dust in the basement or garage. Often, you'll see a frame or wheel just abandoned in a vacant lot. If your town has trash collections you can cruise your neighborhood before the garbage men come. Some towns have a yearly "nuisance removal day," usually in the spring, when the garbage men will haul off things too big for the normal weekly pickup. This gets a lot of people doing a major garage or basement cleanup, and yields the best pickings. A warning about this kind of scavenging: Even though the law says that when someone puts trash out by the road for pickup they give up ownership of it, many people understandably are upset by kids, or adults for that matter, rummaging through it. So do your spotting casually, from a distance, then move in fast, being careful not to make a mess, and leave quickly. Don't hang around picking it over! If they're standing on their lawn, or watching, you'd better ask politely first. Tell them you want to recycle that old frame or wheel and they'll probably be glad to let you have it. If that doesn't work, and there's an especially good prize at stake, you can try waiting at a distance until the garbage truck comes, and ask the garbage man if you can have it.

For smaller parts most bicycle stores usually have a box of used parts they'll sell cheaply if you ask. Anyway, the idea is not to be in a big hurry and rush off to a bike store and pay top dollar, but to look around and get a good deal.

What Kind of Bike to Use

Ten-speeds are nice but aren't being thrown out in any quantity yet. So for most uses a three-speed English bike is best. The frames are light enough for pleasant riding and strong enough to hold up if used in a tandem. And best of all, there are a lot of them around to be found for nothing now that the ten-speed and moto-cross-look bikes, depending on where one's head is, are the "in" things.

Old American bikes, on the other hand, are not worth doing much with for serious riding, but are perfectly good as all-purpose thief-proof (no one would want to take them) "clunkers" and any number of oddball devices. With their cast-iron-like frames, they make a great tandem or sidecar rig where strength, not lightness, is important. They are also, thanks to their wide bars, upright riding position and reliability, the best newspaper-route bikes ever—if your route isn't too hilly. By American, I don't mean just any made-in-the-U.S.A. bike, but the balloon-tired single-speed monsters. But don't be in too much of a hurry to chop one up. The really outrageous ones, with fake gas tanks and springer forks are catching on again. In good shape they're valuable collector bikes, besides being great fun to ride. (There's even a newsletter for clunker freaks—*Classic Bicycle and Whizzer News*, Box 765, Huntington Beach, California 92648.)

There are also many good lightweight English-style three-speed American bikes, so consider these English for the sake of classification and use. But don't forget that the thread sizes may be different (see Threads, page 87).

Buying Parts

Even the very best of scavengers can't always turn up everything they need. Sooner or later you'll need some new parts. The golden rule on buying parts is: Always take the old one along, or if you don't have the old one, take whatever it attaches to. This saves you from going into a shop to buy a bearing or something and finding they come in dozens of sizes and all you can tell the salesperson is, "Well, it's round and shiney, and fits a red bicycle." It'll also keep you on the good side of the people in the shop who get sick of trying to guess what people need. Likewise, know the proper name of the part and they'll take you more seriously.

Secondly, if you need a small part, a pedal bearing, for example, and a shop tells you no one carries it, and you'll have to buy an entire new pedal assembly, don't be discouraged. Try another shop. Some places intentionally don't stock smaller parts so they can sell more big ones. But a good shop, even if they don't have it in stock, will usually be able to find one for you in the junk box.

Also, when you need parts start by finding a real bike shop, not a discount house, a toy shop, or department store with a bike department, but a bike shop with a real parts-and-service department in back. It'll not only be more likely to have what you need, but will be run by people who know what they're talking about and both like and live cycles, not just sell them. This goes double if you ever decide to buy a brand new bike. The bicycle store won't sell you junk, as a lot of the other kinds of stores selling cycles will.

Junk and secondhand stores are also good places to look for all sorts of used parts. Be warned though: The proprietors are usually skilled at getting the best price possible out of you (see Bargaining, page 96).

Wherever you buy, don't be pushed around. Some places will try it just because you're young. Never feel you have to buy something. It's perfectly acceptable to ask the price and look over something and not buy even if the shop people had to dig it out to show you. It's not polite to do this too often at the same place without buying something occasionally, but if a shopkeeper gets mad the first time, just cross his shop off your list.

Building Things

Building things yourself is always most fun when you're building something you couldn't get any other way and something you can really use. I've tried to put only projects like that in this book: things that don't exist if you don't make them yourself or things that are too expensive for most of us to buy.

You will find that building goes a lot smoother if you ask yourself two questions before starting a project: Can you really build it yourself? Can you use it once it's built?

Reading the directions through carefully before starting will help answer the first question. If there's any part of it that's beyond you, line up some help before starting. Help can come from a parent, a friend, or an older (or younger, for that matter) brother or sister. It doesn't matter who, as long as you think you can work it out between you. Sometimes it'll just be a matter of getting something explained to you in more detail than this book does. You probably know someone who is good at building things and can help you out.

A Warning About Adults

Adults know a great deal. However, there is even more they don't know, and they sometimes don't know that they don't know it. So, often they'll try to advise you on something they really know nothing about. If you doubt what they say, they can become annoyed, like when you try to buy something and a salesperson will ask what you need it for and then tell you it won't work. This means that if you go ahead and buy it, it's as good as telling him he doesn't know what he's talking about. The important thing is to remember that those adult advisors may not know any more than you. So don't be buffaloed into doing something their way or not attempting something at all because someone told you it won't work. Find out for yourself!

If the directions are followed, all the projects in this book will work. I know it because I've built them all. It's possible they could be improved on, but the odds are just as good that any changes will have the opposite effect. So have confidence in this book, and in yourself. You'll be O.K.

By the second question—Can you use it once it's built?—I mean do you really have any use for the finished product? Don't build a tandem if you don't have any friends you like to go bike riding with, or a three-wheeler if you're living in the city and have no place to keep it.

The projects in this book fall into three groups: the easy ones, the trickier ones, and then a few you're-on-your-own projects. Some of these call for several bikes' worth of bits and pieces, and you'll end up with a machine you might have little use for. So be realistic! Don't set your heart on building one of the difficult projects first, even though you don't have any of the stuff needed, then drive yourself crazy running around trying to locate everything quickly.

Old parts, you'll find, always seem to come out of hiding when you're not really looking for them. Take your time, grab everything that turns up, and when you've got a good pile of old bikes and parts, that's the time to start building. Or try one of the easier projects first. It will take less time and be more useful.

Using This Book

In the back of this book there is a lot of basic information on making bikes work right without buying fancy tools or new parts, and on how to do the trickier stuff—bending, drilling, and improvising—that the more difficult projects require. Since most of this information is needed for several of the projects, and you may know some of it already, it's been put in the back of the book where you can look it up when you need it.

Usually the page to turn to for more detailed information will be given right in the project. For example, when something needs welding you'll see "(see Welding, page 95)". Or if the page isn't given there you can turn to the table of contents on pages iii–iv and look up Welding.

If you need information on a specific part of the bike the Parts of the Bike diagram on the next page is labeled so that even if you don't know the proper name of the part, you can find it on the diagram, which will tell you where to look for more information.

This way you can plunge full steam ahead into any of the projects without rehashing a lot of stuff you know already. But help is there if you need it—just the thing for people (like me) who hate to read instructions.

When materials for a project are listed, don't feel you have to go by the list exactly. Make any substitutions that'll make it easier or cheaper for you—within reason. For example, if the list calls for 1/2-inch plywood, and you've got some 5/8-inch someone was throwing out, use it. But if it's ¼-inch you've got, it might be pressing your luck to use it. Likewise, if you've got a box of 1-1/2" × 8 wood screws, and the plans call for 1-1/2" × 10, don't go running off to the hardware store.

PARTS OF THE BIKE

All the parts of the bike have their own proper names, which are used throughout this book. Try to learn and use them. Not only because this book won't make any sense to you if you don't, but because it will speed things up when you're trying to bum some free advice at the local bike shop. The page numbers after the part names tell you where to look to find out more about that part.

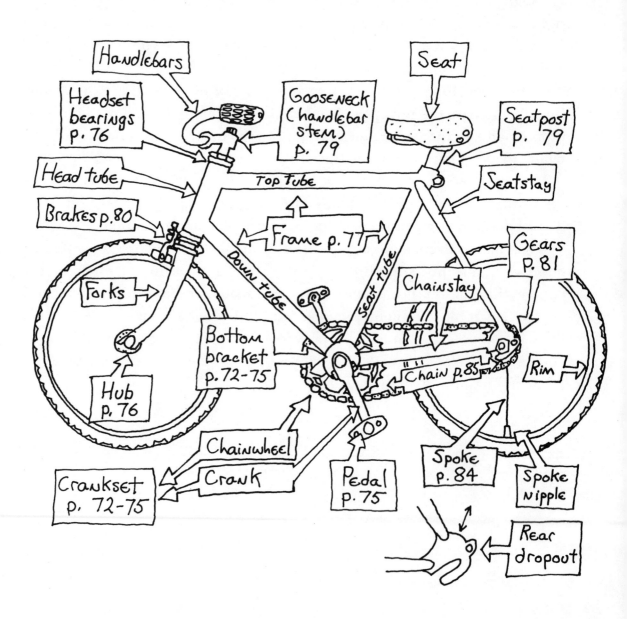

1. RACER

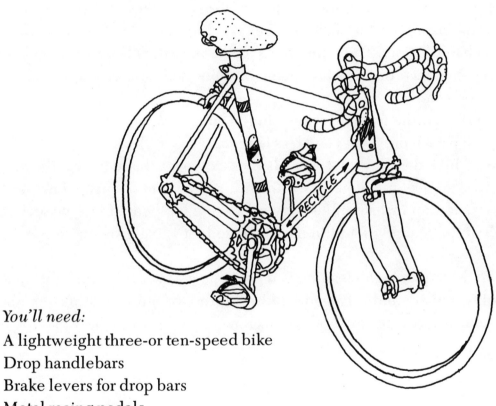

You'll need:
A lightweight three-or ten-speed bike
Drop handlebars
Brake levers for drop bars
Metal racing pedals
Toe clips and straps
Cloth handlebar tape

Tools:
Basic tools (see page 67)

Although the ten-speed fad has taught some people to appreciate good bikes, it has also helped sell a lot of lousy ten-speeds. A racing bike isn't just a bicycle with fancy gears; it's a machine made to get the most possible speed and distance out of the pedaling effort you put into it. It does this by letting you use muscles and techniques most bike riders have never even heard of. Since these techniques depend as much on how the bike is set up as on how it's built, most of them can be applied to any bike to make it outride a badly set up bike that costs three or four times as much!

Here's why. When you ride a regular bike your legs go up and down pushing the pedals on the down stroke. The legs take turns, each working less than half the time. They can't push too hard, or they'll lift your body off the seat. And since the legs are cramped, they can't stretch out to deliver their full power.

If the bike lets the feet and body join in and allows the legs to work their best, you'll have more power and less fatigue.

A racing bike does just that. It coils the body over the legs like a spring, and fastens the feet to the pedals with clips so they can be pushed forward, backward, and up instead of just down. Moving the pedal from the arch to the ball of the foot gives additional leverage that's like growing four more inches of leg.

Add to this a thorough cleaning and greasing and while you're at it some new paint, and any old salvaged junkyard three- or ten-speed bike can be turned into an efficient, good riding machine.

Start by dismantling the bike and going over its bearings, cleaning, greasing, and adjusting them (see Bearings pages 70–76). If you plan to clean the chrome and paint the frame do it now (see pages 94–95).

Now for the important part:

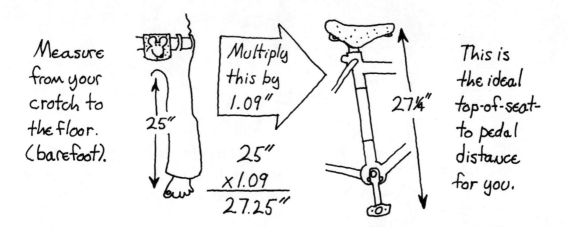

Measure from your crotch to the floor. (barefoot).

25"

Multiply this by 1.09"

25"
x 1.09
27.25"

27¼"

This is the ideal top-of-seat-to pedal distance for you.

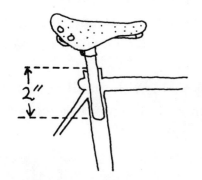

2"

You should always leave at least 2 inches of seat post in the frame tube. If you can't, use a longer post. You really need a bigger frame. But, since they don't turn up at the dump very often, you may have to make the best of what you've got.

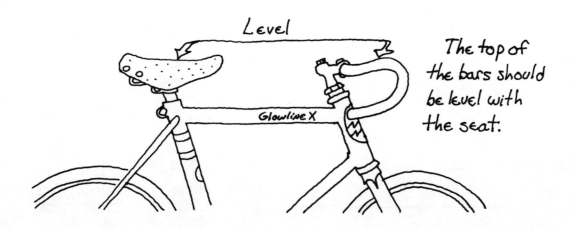

Level

Glowline X

The top of the bars should be level with the seat.

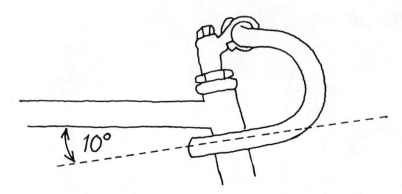

10°

The bars should be set so that the straight lower ends angle slightly downward.

Brake lever position is a matter of personal preference. Try them as pictured here for a start and see how they work out. Don't tape the bars yet.

Although a big rider really needs a larger frame, there are a few ways to stretch a standard bike for more room.

LOOSEN clamp

Most seat frames allow several inches of adjustment back and forth.

A longer gooseneck will move the bars out for more armroom.

Toe clips are one of the speed secrets of a fast bike. Don't try to get away without them. They make a big difference, not only because they keep your feet on the pedals so you can concentrate on pedaling, but because they let you use a bike racer's technique called *ankling*.

The aim of ankling is to use lots of ankle movement to let the legs push effectively on the pedals through as much of the crank's rotation as possible, instead of just stomping on them during the downstroke. Using the clips it's possible to push the pedal forward at the top of the stroke and backward at the bottom. The result? Less wasted energy and more power to the wheel.

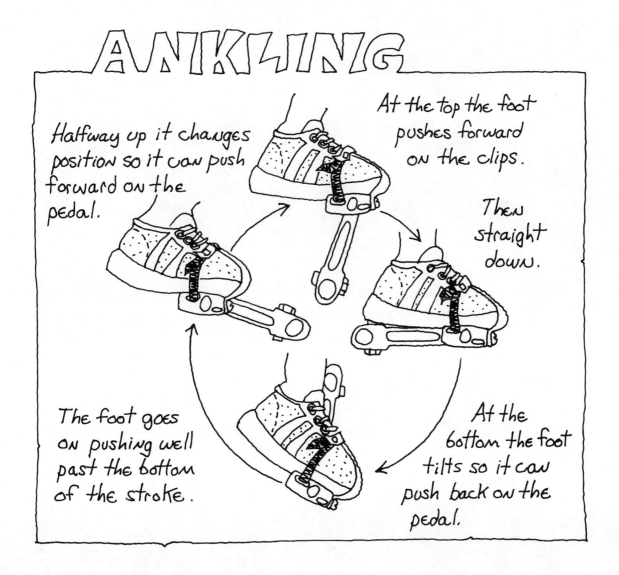

ANKLING

At the top the foot pushes forward on the clips.

Then straight down.

Halfway up it changes position so it can push forward on the pedal.

The foot goes on pushing well past the bottom of the stroke.

At the bottom the foot tilts so it can push back on the pedal.

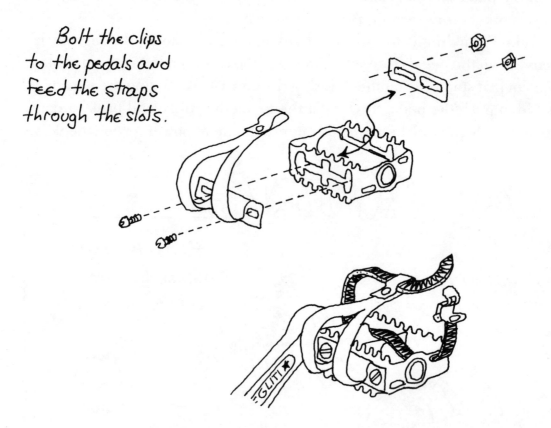

Bolt the clips
to the pedals and
feed the straps
through the slots.

Be sure your tires have enough air in them. Soft tires gobble up energy like crazy, slowing you down and tiring you out unecessarily. And air is free! How much your tires need depends on their size: 26-inch tires (English three-speeds) take 45 pounds per square inch; 27-inch tires (ten-speeds) take 80 pounds per square inch.

If you take bike riding seriously you should get in the habit of checking your tire pressure frequently. If you're really serious, check it every day you ride.

Start with a double
layer by the gooseneck.

Your bike is now set up "by the book," the way racers set up theirs. Try it for a few days like this, no matter how strange it feels at first, then make any changes you feel are necessary. While you're trying it, experiment with the position of the brake levers to get it just right. Once you're happy with the brake levers, tape the handlebars. Cloth tape, from a real bike shop, not only looks better than the plastic stuff department stores sell, but also gives a better and safer grip.

Wrap the bars,
overlapping the tape ⅛" to ¼".

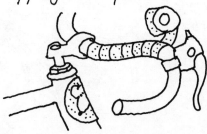

Bring the tape
around the brake lever
to make a tight "V" on
each side, covering it
as closely as possible.

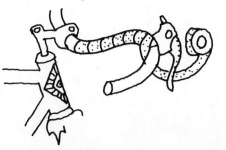

Then
finish
wrapping
the bars.

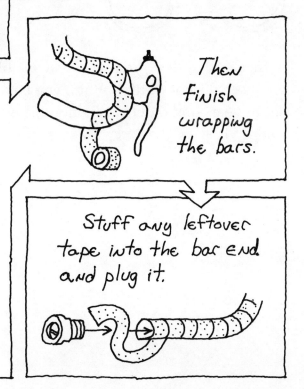

Stuff any leftover
tape into the bar end
and plug it.

Should You Try to Convert a Three-Speed to a Ten-Speed?

Probably not, at least not until you've acquired most of the parts you'll need. Why? The parts you'll need make up a long list, and most of them are expensive. Unless you've got a good head start it would be cheaper to buy a used ten-speed.

The crankset must be replaced, unless you're willing to settle for five speeds, in which case you can get away with filing the teeth on the chainwheel to fit the narrower dérailleur chain. You'll need a rear wheel and sprocket cluster, gears, and levers, and, if you want your front wheel to match the rear, a new front wheel and tire. Cost? At least eighty dollars.

In short, unless you've got a usable set of ten-speed wheels and a crankset, it's not worth it. But if you have these things, the addition of a good set of gears and a decent frame will make as good a bike as you'll find for under $125.

2. BMX BIKE

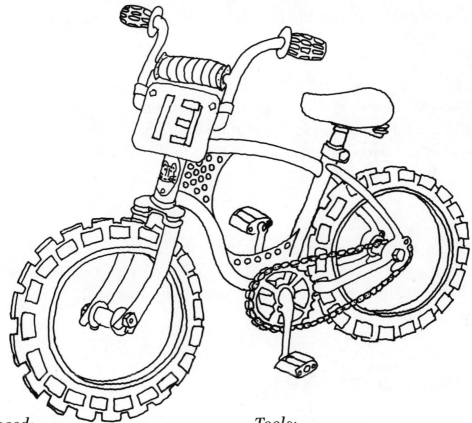

You'll need:
20-inch boy's frame, forks, and wheels
Crankset from a full-sized frame
Seat
Knobby tires
BMX handlebars

And maybe:
Heavy-duty spokes and nipples
Tape, nuts and bolts, paint, etc.
16-guage steel

Tools:
Basic tools (see page 67)

And maybe:
Hacksaw
Drill
Saber saw

Like their motocross motorcycle namesakes, BMX bicycles are built for riding in the dirt. Dirt riding, with its bumps and jumps, is harder on a bike than any other form of cycling, so it's not surprising that an BMX bike can cost as much as a good ten-speed.

But there's another side to the BMX fad. All the bike companies and chain stores have come up with "BMX look" bikes. These look tough with knobby tires and number plates, but have little tags on them stating "Not for off road use or stunting."

If you don't have $150 for a real BMX bike, and don't want a mickey-mouse one, you'll have to build one yourself.

There are two ways you can go about it. If you're not fussy, you can throw together a ride-it-until-it-breaks dirt bike, and have a lot of fun until it does break, or you can take a little more time to build a really rugged one.

The first step is to clean and grease all the bearings. While you've got the crankset apart replace the 5-1/2-inch kiddy crankset on the 20-inch frame with a 6-1/2-inch crankset of the same type that your frame uses (see Cranksets, page 72).

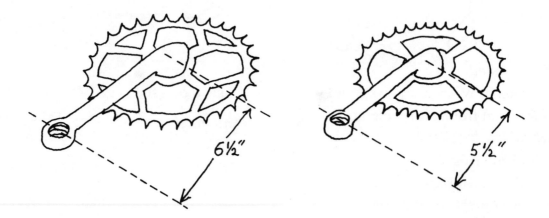

This is one of the secrets of a good BMX bike. The 6-1/2-inch crank gives better leverage for faster take-offs and more climbing power.

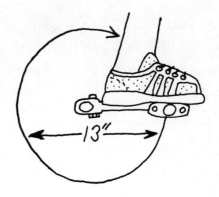

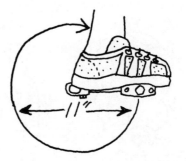

It also reduces ground clearance, so watch it!

Dirt bikes need low gearing, so you'll want a smaller chainwheel than a 6-1/2-inch crankset usually comes with (see Gear ratios, page 86).

The easiest way to get around this is to find a ten-speed crankset with double chainwheels, and just use the smaller one.

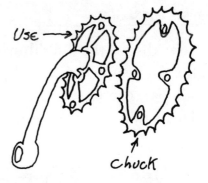

Use →

chuck

If you don't have a spare ten-speed crankset on hand you can graft together the two you have by hacksawing off both chainwheels and bolting the small one from the kiddy crankset onto the center of the full-sized crankset.

Chainwheel cut from the 5½" crankset.

Center "spider" from 6½" crankset.

NOTE! Think before you cut these! Leave as much overlap as possible.

Put them both together, line them up carefully, and drill through where they overlap. Then bolt them together.

Use ¼" or ³/₁₆" bolts if they'll fit, or else whatever you can fit in.

Now throw the knobbies on the wheels, give the spokes a good tightening, and bolt on the handlebars. The crossbar on some M-X handlebars can be a real tooth-breaker, so it should be padded. Some tape and foam rubber scraps from an old cushion will take care of this.

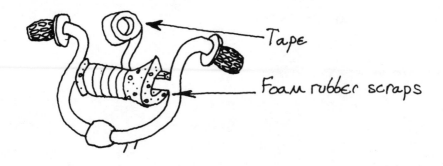

Tape

Foam rubber scraps

If you want a number plate make it the way motorcycle racers do when they're broke.

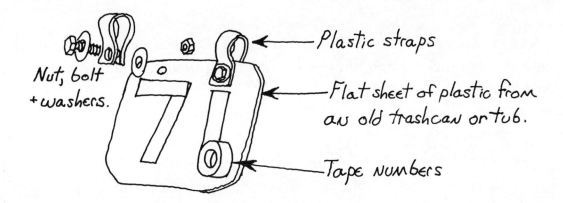

Nut, bolt + washers.

Plastic straps

Flat sheet of plastic from an old trashcan or tub.

Tape numbers

Since flat black paint is all the rage on dirt motorcycles, you've got a fast cure for rusted or pitted chrome—paint it black!

Since paint doesn't like to stick to chrome, use some sandpaper to really rough it up first.

If you want something really different try Wrinkle Finish paint. Get it at a good hardware or paint store, and FOLLOW DIRECTIONS CAREFULLY!

TRIC PAIN CO. BLACK WRINKLE

Any seat is fine, especially because good BMX riding technique involves standing most of the time. Give everything a final tightening and your ride-it-until-it-breaks BMX bike is ready to go.

Now, if you've ridden it and it did break, or if you just want to do things right the first time around, there are a few things you can do to strengthen the bike.

GUSSETS

Gussets are sheet metal reinforcements welded to the frame. The place that needs gusseting most is the head tube, but it's worth doing around the bracket too.

1. Make a cardboard pattern first; then cut the gussets from 16 gauge or so steel sheet with a hacksaw or electric sabre saw.

2. File or grind the gussets to get a snug fit.

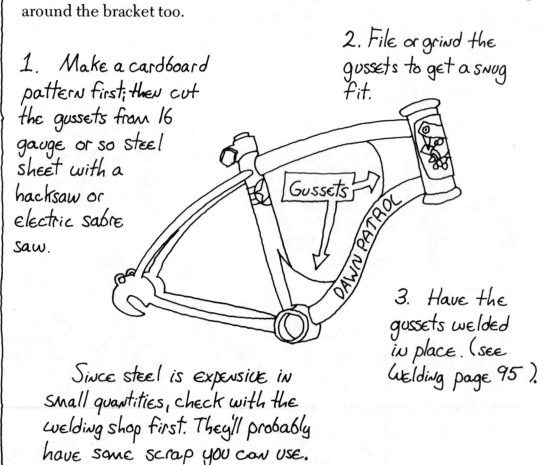

Gussets

DAWN PATROL

3. Have the gussets welded in place. (see welding page 95)

Since steel is expensive in small quantities, check with the welding shop first. They'll probably have some scrap you can use.

SWISS CHEESE

You can give your frame a "trick" look by drilling lightening holes in the frame.

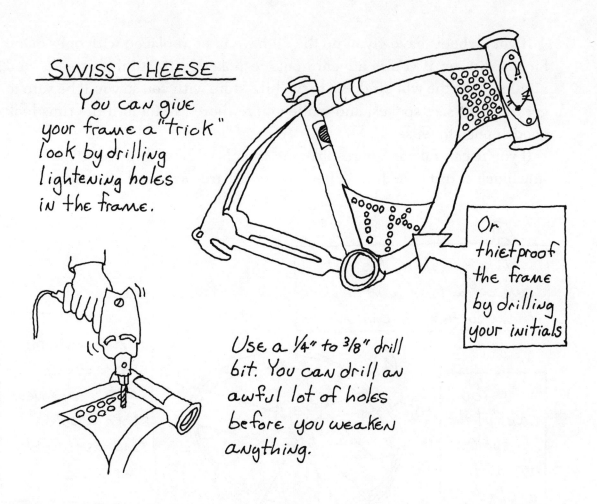

Or thiefproof the frame by drilling your initials

Use a 1/4" to 3/8" drill bit. You can drill an awful lot of holes before you weaken anything.

The forks can be replaced with a pair made especially for dirt riding, or reinforced with a gusset.

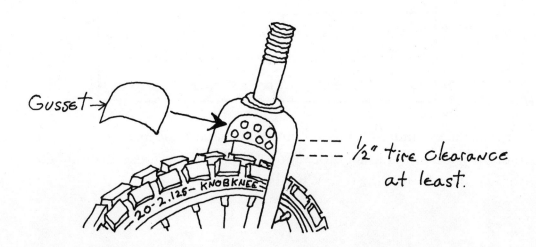

Gusset→

1/2" tire clearance at least.

20-2.125- KNOBKNEE

If your wheels have given up they'll have to be replaced with ones made for the dirt, or, if you're adventurous, respoked with stronger spokes and nipples. Take the wheels down to the bike store with you so you'll be sure to get the right size spokes, and while you're there ask them if the rims look good enough to reuse.

If you're careful you can respoke the wheels without throwing them out of line much. A dirt bike doesn't need wheels as true as a road bike anyway.

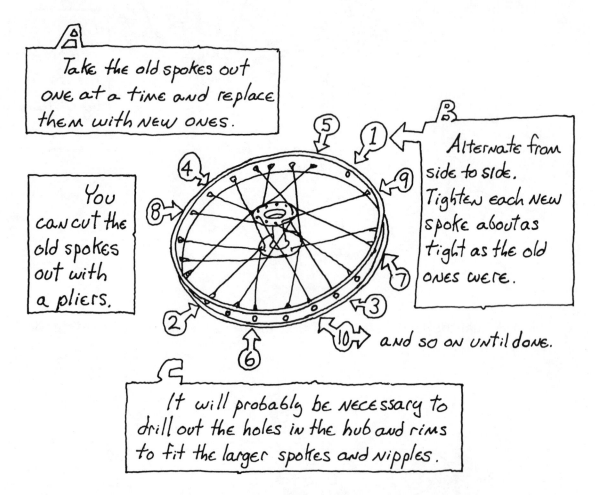

Take the old spokes out one at a time and replace them with new ones.

You can cut the old spokes out with a pliers.

Alternate from side to side. Tighten each new spoke about as tight as the old ones were.

and so on until done.

It will probably be necessary to drill out the holes in the hub and rims to fit the larger spokes and nipples.

If the wheels must be taken completely apart the trick is to do one at a time, using the other as a guide, and assemble them loosely, then take them to a bike shop for trueing (see Wheels, page 84).

3. SKI BIKE

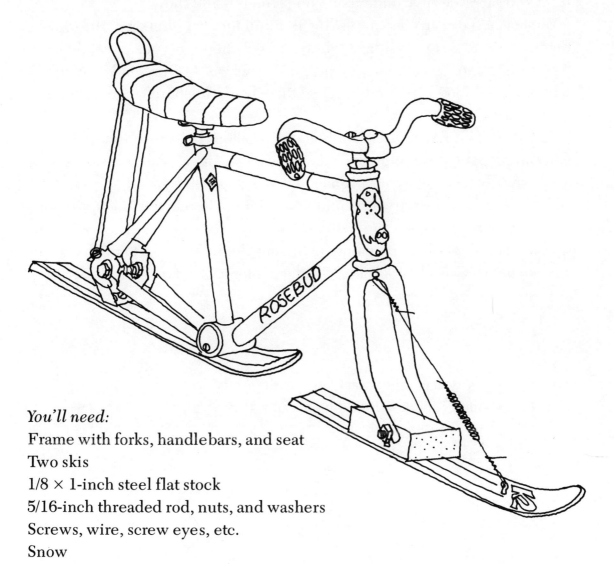

You'll need:
Frame with forks, handlebars, and seat
Two skis
1/8 × 1-inch steel flat stock
5/16-inch threaded rod, nuts, and washers
Screws, wire, screw eyes, etc.
Snow

Tools:
Basic tools (see page 67)
Electric drill
Hacksaw

This ski bike steers like a bike and gives a spectacular ride. Store-bought ones like it are used all over Europe on the ski slopes, and sell for over $100, so it's not just a kiddy toy. It's not very good on unpacked snow because the front end can nose-dive under and dump you into the snow.

Since you'll be carrying or pushing it uphill for every time you ride down, the trick is to keep it light. You're in luck here, because inexpensive American frames (see Frames, page 77), such as Murray and Columbia, which are too shoddy to use for a good bike, work fine here where lightness, not strength, is what matters.

You should have no trouble finding old skis. Skis become obsolete fast, so you can probably find some in a friend's garage. Check with ski stores, too. They usually have a pile of mismatched skis and will be glad to give you a couple. As a last resort try a second-hand store, where a few dollars should buy you a pair. Since they don't have to match, anything will do. (Remember this when bargaining. Mismatched skis aren't much use to anyone but you.) Broken skis are fine, too, as long as the tip ends are usable.

Cut the skis down. The exact length depends on your frame, but for a full-sized frame 27 inches should be about right.

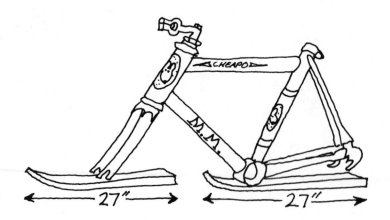

The front ski must be mounted on the end of the forks so it can swivel up and down.

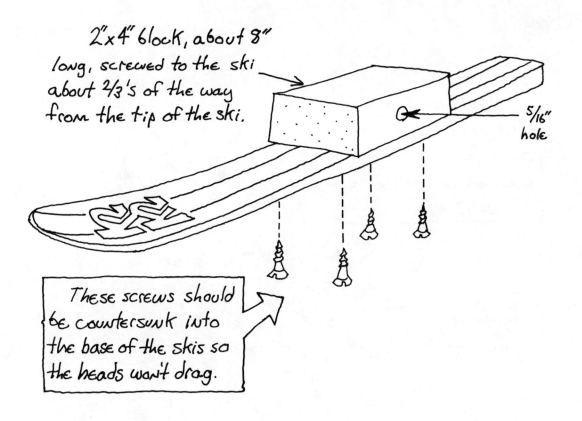

2"x4" block, about 8" long, screwed to the ski about ⅔'s of the way from the tip of the ski.

5/16" hole

These screws should be countersunk into the base of the skis so the heads won't drag.

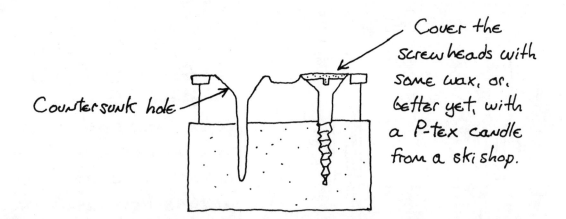

Countersunk hole

Cover the screw heads with some wax, or, better yet, with a P-tex candle from a ski shop.

Bolt the fork ends to a wooden block with a piece of 5/16-inch threaded rod.

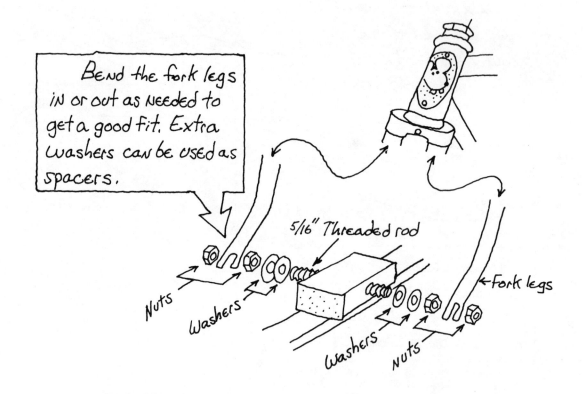

Bend the fork legs in or out as needed to get a good fit. Extra washers can be used as spacers.

5/16" Threaded rod

Nuts

Washers

Fork legs

Washers

Nuts

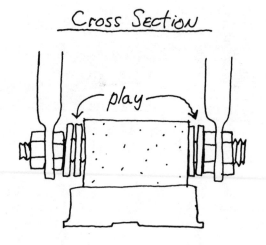

Cross Section

play

Tighten the nuts against the fork ends, not the block. There should be a little play between the washers so the ski can swing up and down, but not so much play that it wobbles from side to side.

Set the bike on a flat surface with both skis in place.

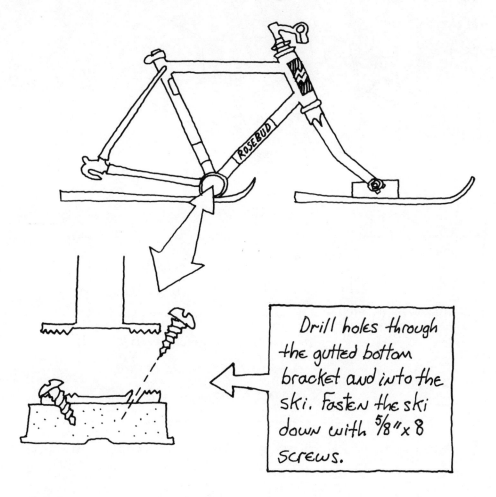

Drill holes through the gutted bottom bracket and into the ski. Fasten the ski down with 5/8" x 8 screws.

The back of the frame will need a mounting bracket since it doesn't touch the ski.

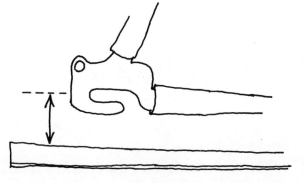

Make the bracket just high enough so both skis lie flat at the same time.

Use a nut and
washer on
each side.

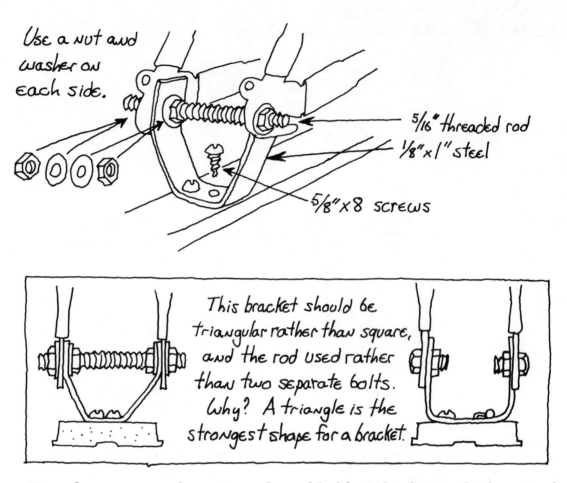

5/16" threaded rod

1/8" x 1" steel

5/8" x 8 screws

This bracket should be
triangular rather than square,
and the rod used rather
than two separate bolts.
Why? A triangle is the
strongest shape for a bracket.

For a footrest use a short piece of wood held on the down tube by a steel bracket.

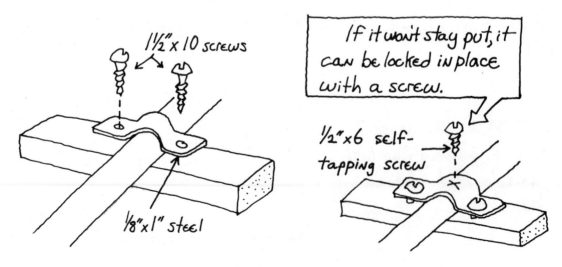

1 1/2" x 10 screws

1/8" x 1" steel

If it won't stay put, it
can be locked in place
with a screw.

1/2" x 6 self-
tapping screw

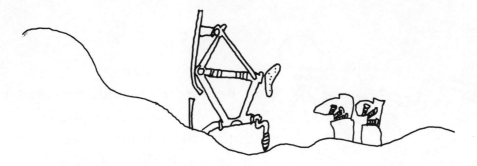

If the tip of the front ski swings down too far it can catch or nose-dive into the snow, bringing the ski bike to a very abrupt stop! Rig a wire to hold the ski at the proper "angle of attack."

Use a spring or some giant rubber bands from an old inner tube as a "shock absorber" so the ski can move enough to follow bumps.

Screw eye →

TURBOT

Any seat will work. A banana seat is nice because it lets you shift your weight around, but it's heavier, too.

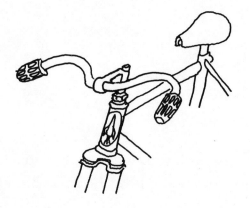

Reverse the handlebars and be sure both ends have proper hand-grips. This is insurance against poking yourself when you wipe out.

Depending on the skis you use you may have problems with the back ski's tip breaking. It can be reinforced with a piece of 1/2-inch or so plywood screwed down between the ski and the frame.

If the front ski mounting block has a tendency to split, a couple of screws through it from the top will hold it together. These don't necessarily even have to reach into the ski.

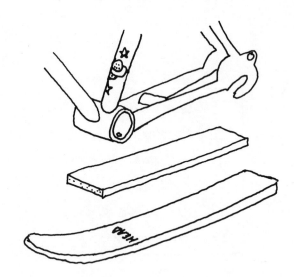

Riding the Ski Bike

It'll take a while to get the knack of riding the ski bike. You wouldn't try to learn to ski by plunging straight down the steepest slope you could find; don't start that way with the ski bike either.

It works best on packed snow, just as skis or runnered Flexible Flyer-type sleds do. In deep snow it will try to throw you over the bars if the front ski catches, and on ice or icy crust it won't steer very well.

Riding it is very much like riding a bike on dirt or gravel. To turn sharply or stop you throw the bike around and lean it hard on its side in a "power-turn" skid. This digs the skis' edges in much the way the back wheel on a bike digs in when you lock the brakes on dirt.

4. EXERCISE BIKE

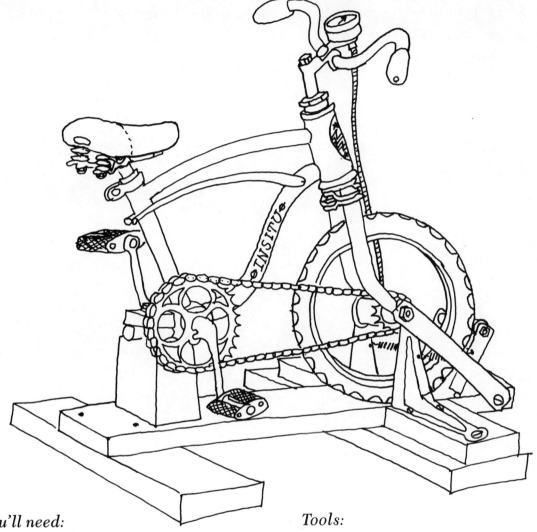

You'll need:
Complete bike minus front wheel
Any size back wheel
2 × 6-inch board, 8 feet long
1/8 × 1-inch steel flat stock
Two 12- or 14-inch shelf brackets
Some two-by-four scraps
Odd nuts, bolts, springs, and bits of pipe.

Tools:
Basic tools (see page 67)
Hacksaw
Drill
Wood saw

Made from a cut-down frame, this is a good way to put a bent frame and forks out to pasture. It's noisy and takes up a lot of room, so figure out where to put it before you get too involved in building it. But, equipped with toe clips it could be just the thing you need to stay in shape when the riding is snowed out. Or you could give it to an overweight parent as a bribe to forgive the pile of junk bike parts under your bed.

The frame is made from an 8-foot two-by-four, and is nailed or screwed together.

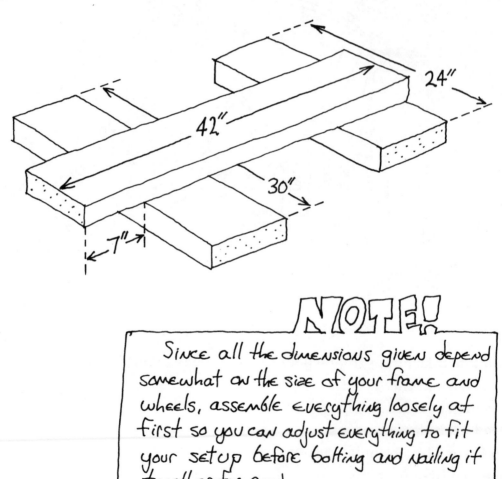

NOTE!

Since all the dimensions given depend somewhat on the size of your frame and wheels, assemble everything loosely at first so you can adjust everything to fit your setup before bolting and nailing it together for good.

Cut the back stays off the frame.

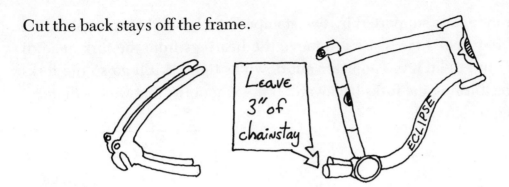

The back of the frame sits on a block of wood. This should be about 12 inches high for a full-sized frame and wheel, or 10 inches for a 20-inch frame.

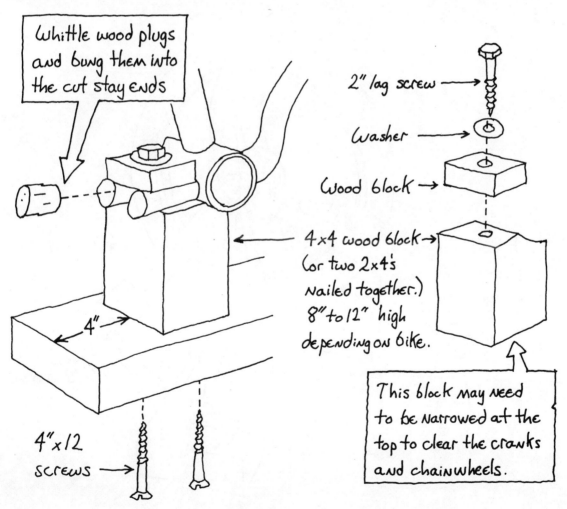

Whittle wood plugs and bung them into the cut stay ends

2" lag screw →

Washer →

Wood block →

4×4 wood block → (or two 2×4's Nailed together.) 8" to 12" high depending on bike.

4"

4"×12 screws →

This block may need to be Narrowed at the top to clear the cranks and chainwheels.

The front end is supported by two stamped steel shelf brackets, steadied by steel flat stock braces. First remove the bearings from the fork head, if possible, and tighten the adjuster nut down as tight as it'll go so the forks can't turn. Turning the forks backward, if the wheel fits that way, will make the rig more compact.

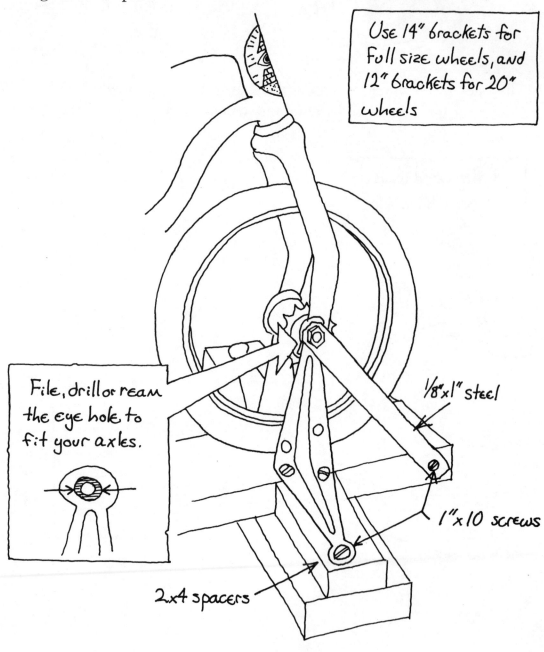

Use 14" brackets for full size wheels, and 12" brackets for 20" wheels

File, drill or ream the eye hole, to fit your axles.

1/8"x1" steel

1"x10 screws

2x4 spacers

A spring-loaded hinged roller on the wheel adds pedaling resistance.

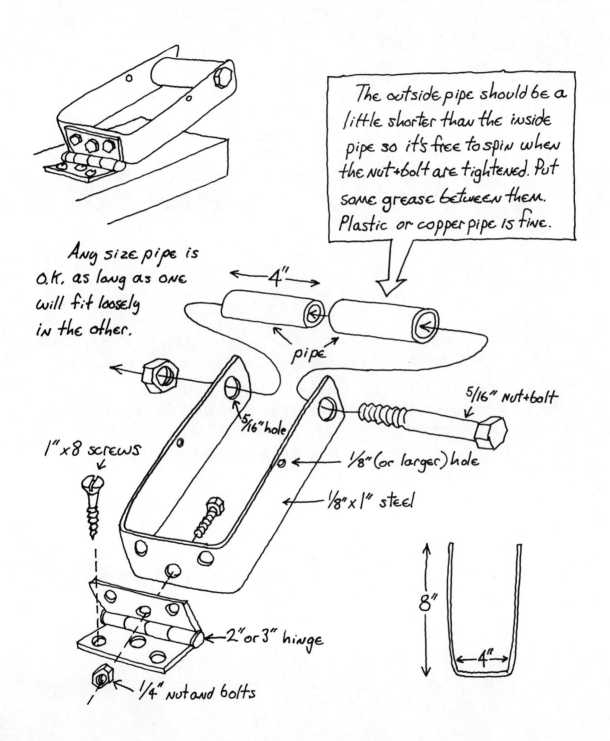

The outside pipe should be a little shorter than the inside pipe so it's free to spin when the nut + bolt are tightened. Put some grease between them. Plastic or copper pipe is fine.

Any size pipe is O.K. as long as one will fit loosely in the other.

4"

pipe

5/16" Nut + bolt

5/16" hole

1/8" (or larger) hole

1" x 8 screws

1/8" x 1" steel

8"

4"

2" or 3" hinge

1/4" Nut and bolts

Screw the roller to the base in front of the brackets. The springs go from each side of the roller frame to the brackets.

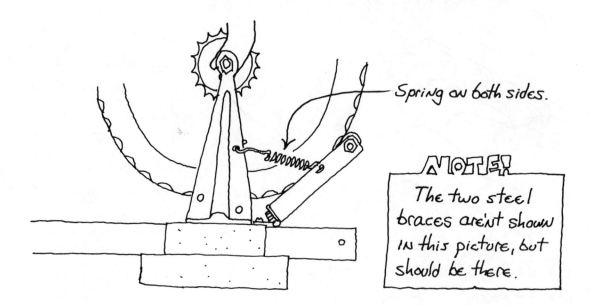

Spring on both sides.

NOTE!
The two steel braces are'nt shown in this picture, but should be there.

Don't go too wild with the spring pressure. The secret to getting in shape for riding is to keep the legs spinning fast without too much resistance rather than plodding along on pedals you can barely turn.

If you've got an old speedometer, and you're too cool to put it on your racer, this is the perfect spot for it. If it has an odometer you can have races with your friends—try timing how long it takes to ride five miles.

5. TANDEM

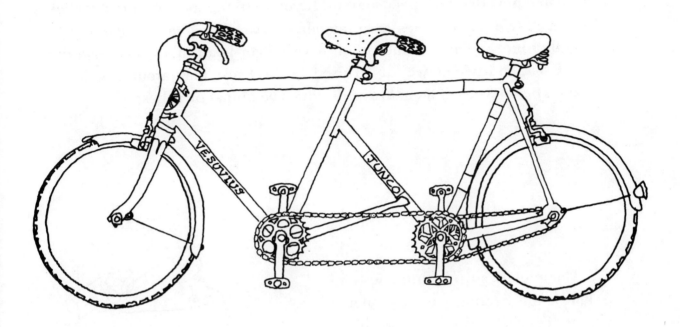

You'll need:
Two bike frames
Two seats and posts
Two handlebars and goosenecks
Two cranksets
Front and back wheels
Spare chain, chainwheel, nuts and bolts, hose clamps, etc.

Tools:
Basic tools (see page 67)
Hacksaw
File

And maybe:
Electric drill

You can make a tandem out of any two bikes as long as they're more or less alike—grafting a balloon-tired clunker to a superlight ten-speed won't make it. English-style three-speeds are the best choice because they're both light enough to ride well, and strong enough to hold up. Best of all they're easily available now that ten-speeds are in. If you're trying to make a really slick job of it, two boy's frames are preferable because they're stronger and fit together nicely. Girl's frames often have longer head tubes that raise the front seat and pedals way up if used in the back. Play around with the frames before you cut them to decide which combination is best.

Completely strip both frames and knock the bearing cups out of the rear frame's head tube. Then hacksaw the head tube in two, down the middle.

Cut the seat stays off the front frame.

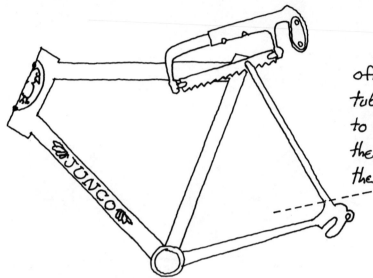

Cut the chainstays off flush with the seat tube, being careful not to cut into it. Then file the cuts smooth. Cut the other above the dropouts.

While English frames will usually fit together perfectly, on some frames it will be necessary to carefully bend the cut sides on the head tube in or out to get a snug fit on the front frame's seat tube.

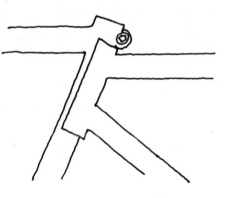

To narrow it, hammer the edges.

A scrap of pipe about the size of the seat tube makes a good tool for shaping the head tube.

To widen, hammer the pipe down in.

Clamp the frames together temporarily with the hose clamps, and bend the chopped-off chainstays so the dropouts meet the back frame's down tube.

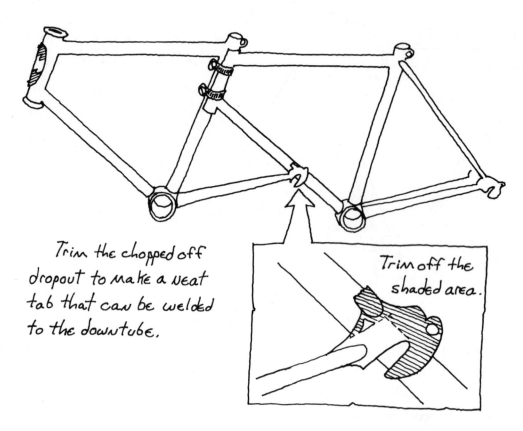

Trim the chopped off dropout to make a neat tab that can be welded to the downtube.

Trim off the shaded area.

The ends of the chainstay should nicely overlap the down tube. If you can bend the tabs to fit the round tube you'll get an even stronger joint.

NO GOOD
No overlap.

O.K.
Good overlap.

BEST!
Curved to fit snug against tube.

File or sand the frames clean to the bare metal where they meet and take them to be welded together (see Welding, page 95).

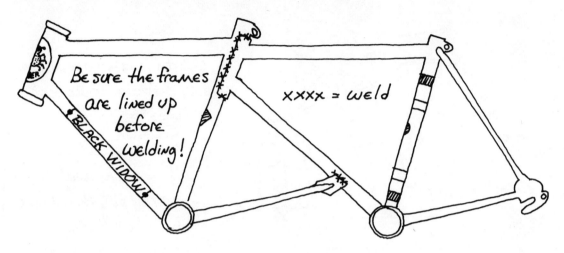

After welding, clean up the welds with sandpaper or a file and wire brush, and the frame is ready to paint (see Paint, page 94). Once the frame is painted you can put the forks, wheels, and brakes back on, and while you're at it, clean, grease, and adjust all the bearings (see pages 70-77).

WARNING!

A tandem carries twice the weight of a solo bike, but it doesn't have any extra wheels to help it along. As a result the wheels and brakes are much more heavily loaded. Use the best wheels you've got, and give the spokes a good tightening. Since the brakes will be working twice as hard, and it's difficult to gracefully coordinate foot dragging with two riders, use a coaster brake on the rear and caliper brakes on both front and back. You'll need a special extra-long cable to reach the back caliper—get it from a bike shop or mail-order house (page 97).

Don't skimp on brakes. A brakeless tandem is a terror on a steep hill. Shortcuts that might get by—for a while—on a solo bike won't work here.

You'll need a combination seat and handlebars for the middle. With luck you can make this with a gooseneck and a seat clamp turned sideways.

You'll probably need some shims (page 94) to get everything to fit.

Pry the clamp open and slip it over the gooseneck.

If the seat won't stay put, the clamp can be locked in place with a ½"x 6 self-tapping metal screw.

If that doesn't work you'll have to have a set of bars welded on to the seat post.

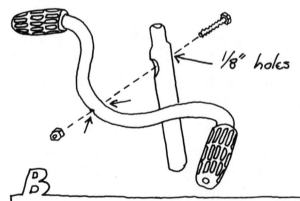

With the seat on the bike, decide where the bars should go, and drill a ⅛" hole through the seatpost at that point. Drill the bars to match.

⅛" holes

File or grind a notch around the hole on the back of the post so the bars fit snugly. Bolt the bars to the post with a good ⅛"x 2" bolt, and have them welded.

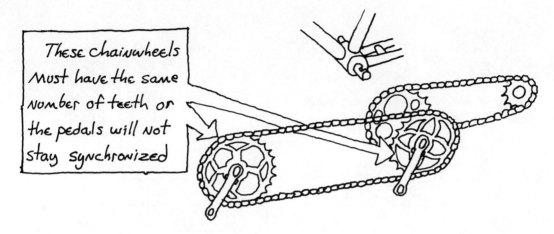

These chainwheels must have the same number of teeth or the pedals will not stay synchronized

Now comes the tricky part. Unless the front rider will be just going along for the ride, the front pedals must be connected to the rear pedals by a second chain. This calls for a double chainwheel on the rear cranks.

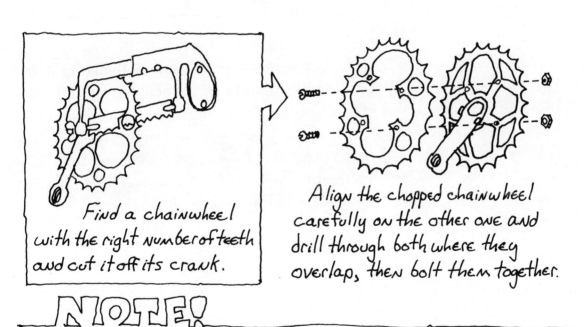

Find a chainwheel with the right number of teeth and cut it off its crank.

Align the chopped chainwheel carefully on the other one and drill through both where they overlap, then bolt them together.

NOTE!

The size and number of bolts needed will depend on how nicely the chainwheels overlap. If you can drill ¼" holes, 4 or 5 bolts will do. If there's not enough space for them, try 8 to 10 ⅛" holes, and use 7-32 or so nuts + bolts, or ⅛" pop rivets.

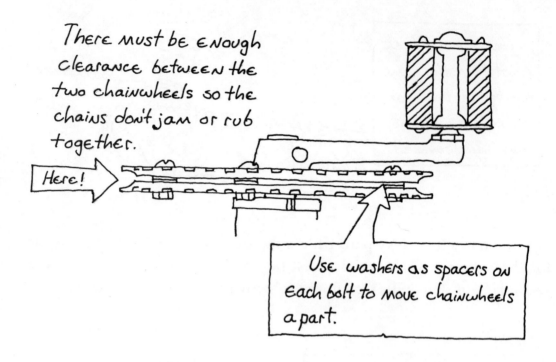

There must be enough clearance between the two chainwheels so the chains don't jam or rub together.

Here!

Use washers as spacers on each bolt to move chainwheels apart.

Make the front chain from the two rears joined together with master links. Play around with the different combinations to get the chains as straight and the chainwheels as much in line as possible. On most three-speed hubs you can move the sprocket in or out about 1/4-inch by moving shims from one side to the other, but other than that there's not much you can do if they don't line up. It's more important to have the front chain aligned than the back, since it can be adjusted only by adding or removing links.

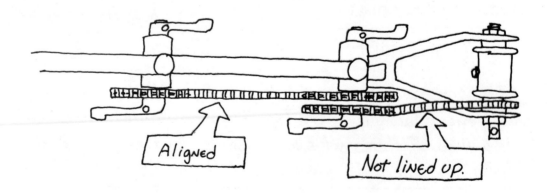

Aligned

Not lined up.

Troubleshooting

If the frame flexes too much, or threatens to break, or if for any reason it'll be carrying an extra heavy load, it can be reinforced.

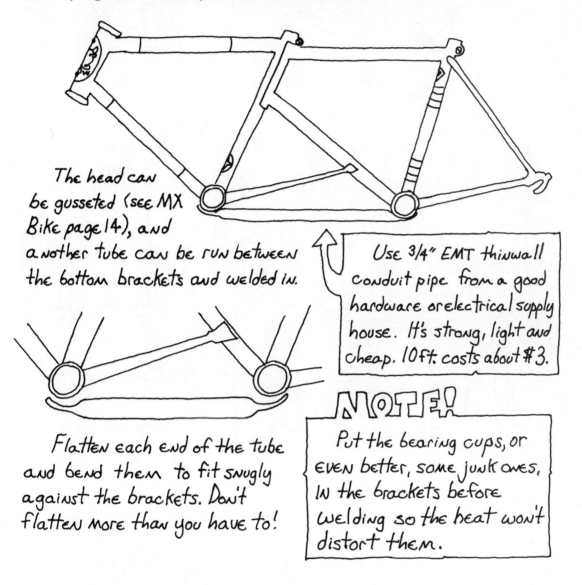

The head can be gusseted (see MX Bike page 14), and another tube can be run between the bottom brackets and welded in.

Use 3/4" EMT thinwall conduit pipe from a good hardware or electrical supply house. It's strong, light and cheap. 10 ft. costs about $3.

Flatten each end of the tube and bend them to fit snugly against the brackets. Don't flatten more than you have to!

NOTE!

Put the bearing cups, or even better, some junk ones, in the brackets before welding so the heat won't distort them.

The front chain may not stay put. You can make a chain adjuster to keep it tight so it won't jump off. This is pretty complicated, though, so save it for a last resort and try first to solve the problem by aligning and adjusting the chain as well as possible.

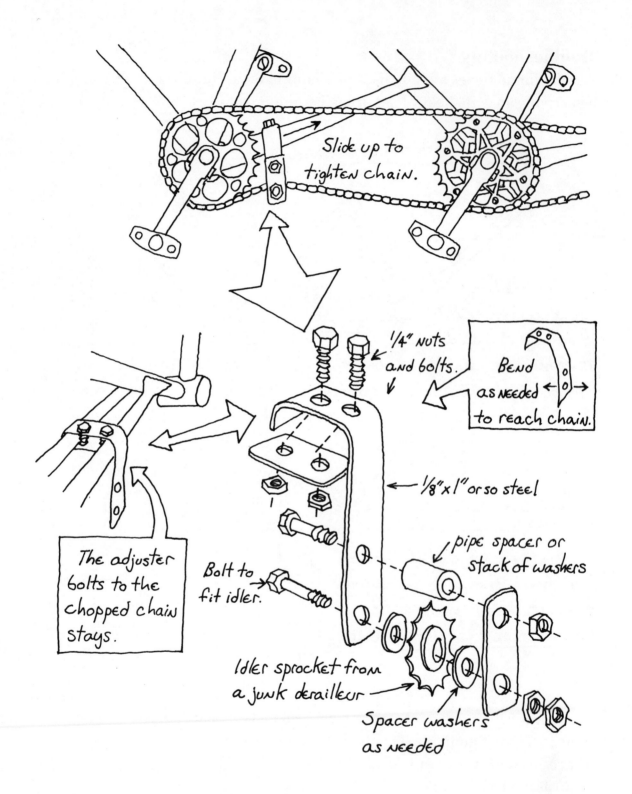

Slide up to tighten chain.

1/4" nuts and bolts.

Bend as needed to reach chain.

1/8" x 1" or so steel

pipe spacer or stack of washers

Bolt to fit idler.

The adjuster bolts to the chopped chain stays.

Idler sprocket from a junk derailleur

Spacer washers as needed

6. THREE WHEELER

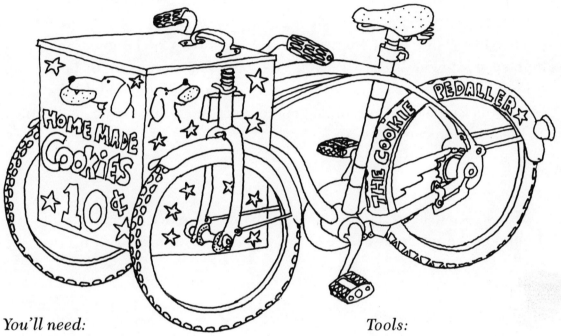

You'll need:
Complete bike with coaster brake back wheel
Two extra front forks
One extra front wheel
Sheet of 1/2-inch plywood
Two 8-foot 2" × 3"'s
Six fender washers
Two eyebolts
Two 1/2-inch conduit clamps
1/8 × 1-1/4-inch angle iron
Odds and ends: nuts, bolts, hinges, etc.

Tools:
Basic tools (see page 67)
Hacksaw
Drill

Three-wheeled bikes are used all over the world as taxis and for light hauling. Once in India I saw one being used in a one-bike funeral procession carrying driver, five passengers, and the corpse. They were heading for Benares, twelve miles down the road. In the U.S. ice-cream bars make up the three-wheelers' heaviest loads. This bike is patterned after those ice-cream-cart bikes.

Begin with the strongest frame you've got. Since it would be just about impossible to synchronize brakes on the front wheels, you'll have to get by with just the one on the back, so you'll need a wheel with a big fat tire and a coaster brake in very good working order.

This bike isn't built for speed, and is not up to hard cornering or high-speed downhill runs. But line the box with styrofoam, or better yet, drop in a foam ice chest, and it'll be perfect for peddling cold drinks or ice cream, or tacos and yogurt, for that matter. Its strange appearance will attract all the attention you'll need!

The steering head angle must be changed so that it's vertical to the ground or the machine will lean the wrong way on turns and tip over too easily.

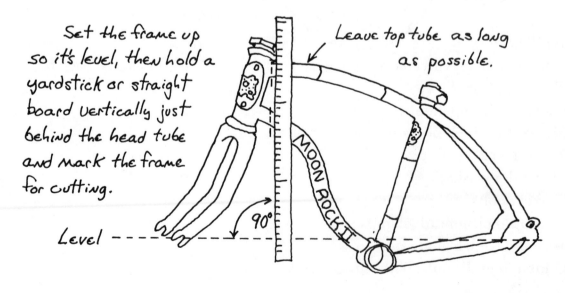

Set the frame up so it's level, then hold a yardstick or straight board vertically just behind the head tube and mark the frame for cutting.

Leave top tube as long as possible.

Level

90°

MOON ROCK II

Hacksaw off both frame tubes where you've marked them.

The cuts must be in line
with each other as marked.

Right

Wrong +
No good.

Then file or grind the cut ends of the frame tubes so they fit against the head tube.

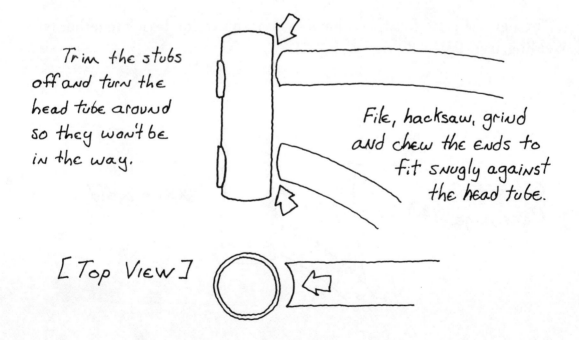

Trim the stubs
off and turn the
head tube around
so they won't be
in the way.

File, hacksaw, grind
and chew the ends to
fit snugly against
the head tube.

[Top View]

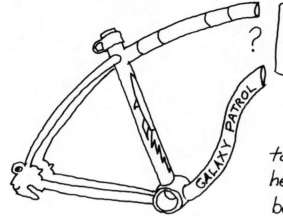

If the frame tubes are too far apart to fit the head tube, they'll have to be bent together a bit.

You can use a couple pieces of pipe slipped over the tubes for more leverage.

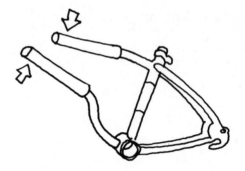

Cut a gusset plate to fit, and have everything welded back together (see Welding, page 95).

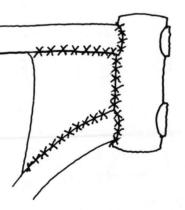

Gusset plate (see page 14)

xxxx = weld

The box is made from 1/2-inch plywood with two-by-threes (or two-by-fours if you've got some lying around) for a frame. Use plywood marked "exterior glue," or it'll come apart in the rain!

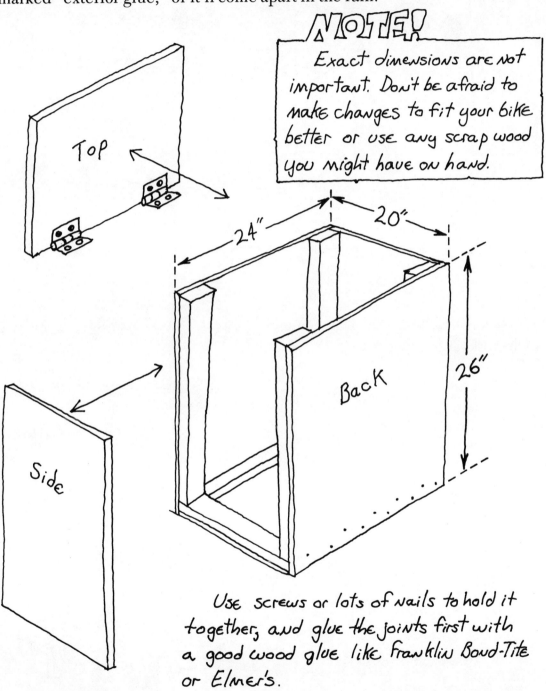

NOTE!

Exact dimensions are not important. Don't be afraid to make changes to fit your bike better or use any scrap wood you might have on hand.

Top

24"

20"

Back

26"

Side

Use screws or lots of nails to hold it together, and glue the joints first with a good wood glue like Franklin Bond-Tite or Elmer's.

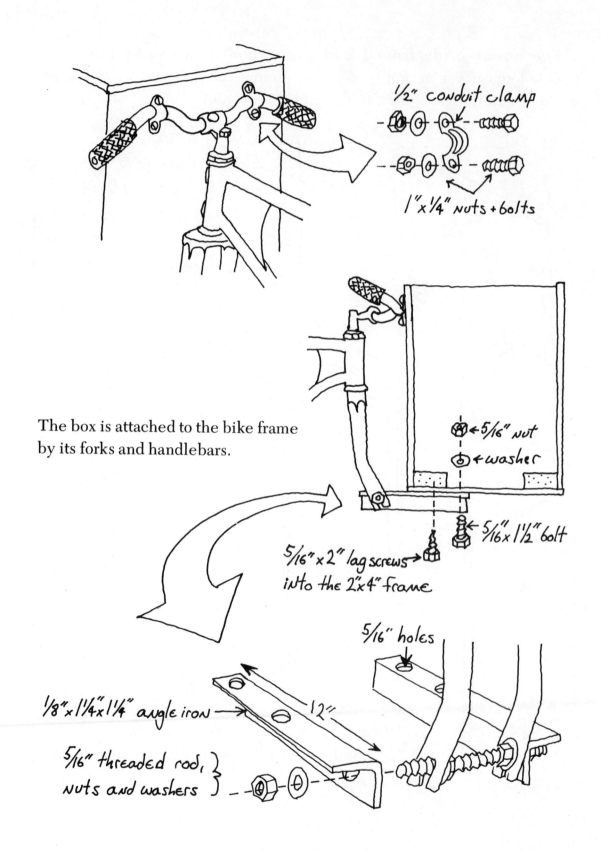

½" conduit clamp

1" x ¼" nuts + bolts

The box is attached to the bike frame by its forks and handlebars.

←5/16" nut

←washer

5/16 x 1½" bolt

5/16" x 2" lag screws→ into the 2"x4" frame

5/16" holes

⅛" x 1¼" x 1¼" angle iron →

12"

5/16" threaded rod, nuts and washers

The two extra forks are bolted on each side of the box.

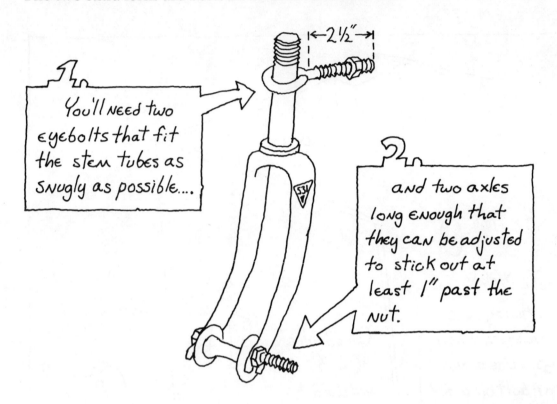

You'll NEED two eyebolts that fit the stem tubes as SNugly as possible....

←—2½″—→

and two axles long ENough that they can be adjusted to stick out at least 1″ past the Nut.

Prop the box up so the bike sits level with the head tube at a right angle to the ground, and drill a 5/16- or 3/8-inch hole, depending on the size of the axle, on each side where the center of the wheel should go.

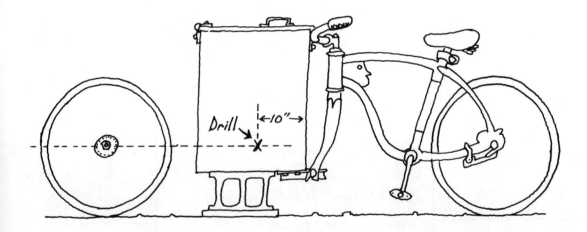

Drill → X   ←—10″—→

Using the forks as a guide, drill another hole in each side for the eyebolts.

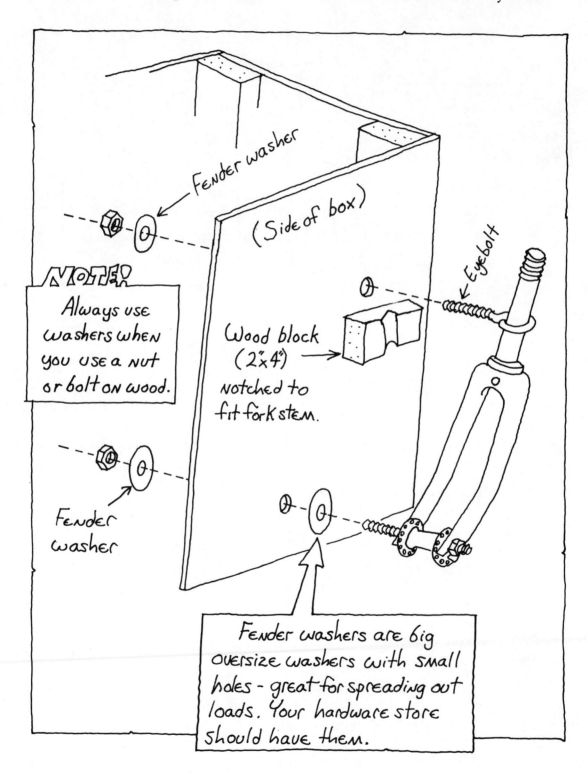

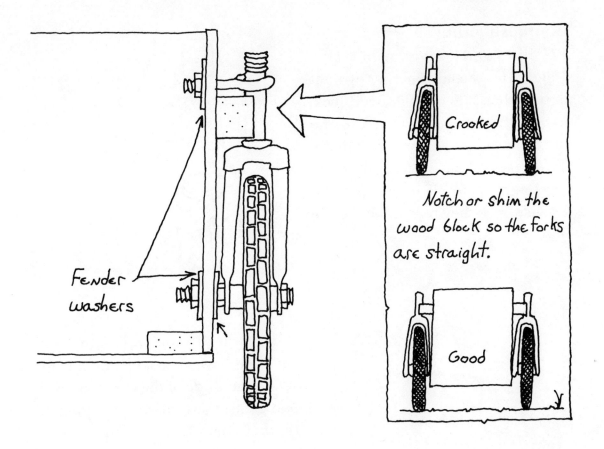

Fender washers

Crooked

Notch or shim the wood block so the forks are straight.

Good

The three-wheeler should now be ready to ride. Depending on the gears used, it may be hard to pedal (see Gear ratios, page 86). Fix this by lowering the ratios, gearing the same way as for the BMX bike (pages 11–12).

If your coaster brake doesn't have enough stopping power add a caliper brake on the back wheel and use both brakes together.

Riding the Three-Wheeler

Like a sidecar rig, the three-wheeler handles completely differently than a two-wheeled bike. It must be steered deliberately, like a car, since it won't lean into turns. This will feel strange at first, so practice in a safe place with no cars and plenty of room.

It isn't built for speed, and will start to feel very spooky if you push it too hard, so take it easy until you get a feel for its limitations. And take it really easy on hills, especially if it's loaded.

Troubleshooting

If the front wheel won't stay straight you can add another eyebolt on the other side of the wood block, or have the eyebolt welded to the fork stem so it can't turn, or do both. If you have them welded, be sure that the bits are all lined up right, because once they're welded they're on to stay!

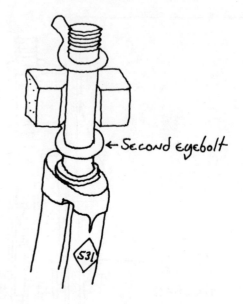

←Second eyebolt

S31

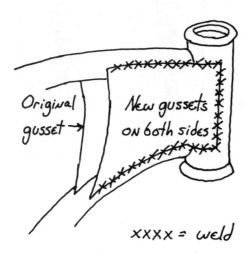

Original gusset →

New gussets on both sides

xxxx = weld

If the head tube welds give you any trouble you can add another gusset on each side of the frame, or even one continuous gusset wrapping all the way around the head tube.

7. SIDECAR RIG

You'll need:
A complete bike
Extra fork and wheel
3 feet of 1/4 × 1-1/4-inch steel flat stock
3 feet of 1/8 × 1-1/4-inch steel flat stock
10 feet of 3/4-inch EMT thinwall electrical conduit
Two 3/4-inch conduit clamps
A 26-inch piece of 2" × 4"
A sheet of 1/2-inch plywood
An 8-foot piece of two-by-three
Nails, screws, nuts, bolts, etc.

Tools:
Basic tools (see page 67)
Hacksaw
Electric drill
Big vise

This sidecar rig is a favorite of mine. It'll do anything the ice-cream-cart three-wheeler will, and it will outride and outhandle it. Best of all, you don't have to butcher a good bike to build it. When you get tired of it you can unbolt the sidecar and still have a solo bike.

While it doesn't require welding, it's trickier to build because it takes some hard bending, and a lot of trial and error to get everything lined up right. But, unless you must have a box-in-front three-wheeler, give this a try first.

Putting a sidecar on a bicycle is difficult because you have to leave room for the pedals to turn, which doesn't leave many places to attach the rig. This design is adapted from a 1919 copy of *The Boy Mechanic* and would be a real knockout hooked up to an old American clunker with spring forks and a fake gas tank. Painted up it would be great advertising for an ecology-minded business.

Start by attaching the extra fork and wheel to the bike's back wheel with a strut. The 1919 version used an elegant truss, but a two-by-four is a lot simpler.

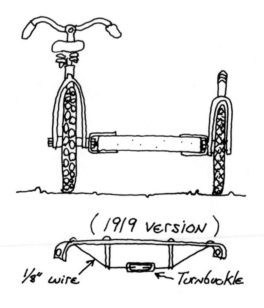

(1919 version)

1/8" wire   ← Turnbuckle

NOTE!

Building this rig requires lots of tricky bending, and a good, big, vise is absolutely necessary. Check around- someone you know probably has one. Or if you're on good terms with a local gas station ask if you can use theirs.

Cut the 3-foot length of 1/4×1-1/4-inch steel in two and bend each piece to fit over the ends of the two-by-four.

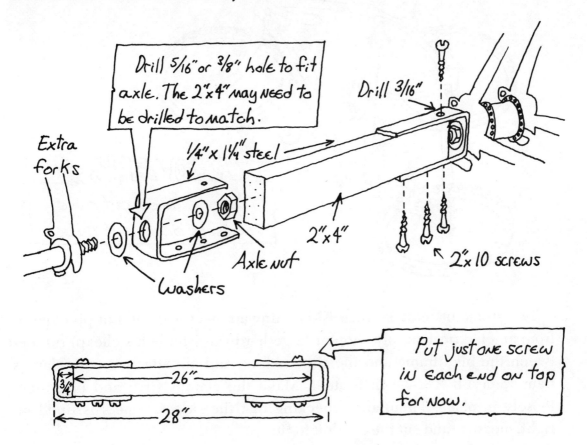

Drill 5/16" or 3/8" hole to fit axle. The 2"x4" may need to be drilled to match.

Drill 3/16"

Extra forks

1/4" x 1¼" steel

2"x4"

Axle nut

Washers

2"x 10 screws

26"

28"

3/4"

Put just one screw in each end on top for now.

Fasten the strut between the two wheels using their axle nuts, and tighten them down so the fork stem is pointing forward at about a 45-degree angle to the ground.

NOTE!
Put the sidecar on the right of the bike so it doesn't stick out into traffic.

45°

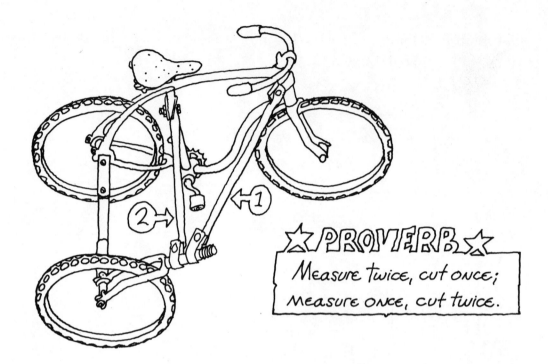

Two struts made of 3/4-inch EMT thinwall electrical conduit pipe (get it from an electrical supply shop or large hardware store—it's cheap) run between the bike frame and the sidecar fork, and are attached with clamps bent from 1/8 × 1-1/4-inch steel. Make the clamps first, and bolt them loosely in place. Then, after checking that the sidecar wheel is lined up right, measure and cut the conduit to fit.

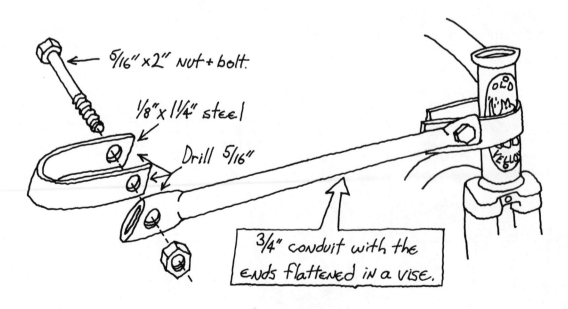

5/16" × 2" Nut + bolt.

1/8" × 1¼" steel

Drill 5/16"

3/4" conduit with the ends flattened in a vise.

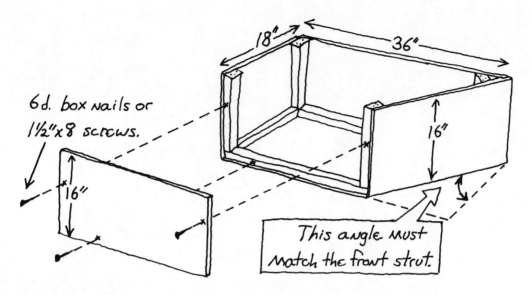

6d. box nails or
1½"x8 screws.

18"

36"

16"

16"

This angle must
match the front strut.

The sidecar body is made of 1/2-inch plywood nailed or screwed to two-by-threes. The front of the box must be angled to match the front strut. The middle strut has to pass through both sides of the box, so when you've got the plywood pieces all cut, assemble the body loosely, minus the two sides, and put it in place on the bike. Carefully measure where the middle strut goes, and cut or drill holes in the sides to match.

A

Use a board held vertically to mark the bottom piece to match the angle of the front strut.

B

Then measure where the middle strut goes and cut the side boards to fit.

Prop it up level!

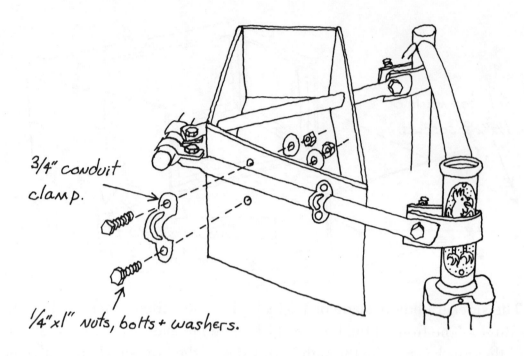

3/4" conduit clamp.

1/4"x1" Nuts, bolts + washers.

Once the body is finished remove the middle strut and fit the body to the frame, then refit the middle strut before fastening the body in place. The front of the body is bolted to the front strut with two 3/4-inch conduit clamps (get these where you get the conduit) and the back is screwed down to the two-by-four axle strut.

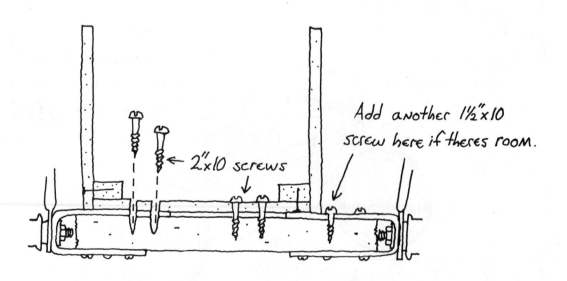

← 2"x10 screws

Add another 1½"x10 screw here if theres room.

Use brackets bent from 1/8×1-1/4-inch steel to fasten the middle strut to the body where it runs through it. Don't forget these, because they stiffen up the rig considerably.

That finishes it, although some paint would look good on the sidecar. You'll probably hav to do some fiddling with the gear ratio (see page 86) to get the rig to pedal easily.

Riding the Sidecar Rig

Riding a sidecar rig is different, to say the least. Steering a regular bicycle is done almost completely with your body. You don't really use the handlebars much, and as often as not they're turned in the opposite direction of the turn (try it if you don't believe me!). There's no such subtlety in steering a sidecar rig. The bars are turned—hard—in the direction you want to go—which is very spooky, because it goes against everything you've ever learned about riding a bike. When the rig corners it doesn't lean, although you can lift the sidecar wheel if you try. If it's cornered too fast it drifts (skids) or flips—just like a motorcycle sidecar! To make it even more confusing it's asymmetrical—the two sides are completely different—so it will behave differently depending on which way you're turning. All this makes riding it very strange at first, and fun!

Troubleshooting

The sidecar wheel may not stay in alignment if the clamps on the fork stem are not a good fit. The surest fix is to have the clamps welded to the stem so it can't twist. If welding isn't available drill through the clamps into the stem with a 1/8-inch drill and use a self-tapping metal screw to pin the stem in position. Be sure it's lined up right first!

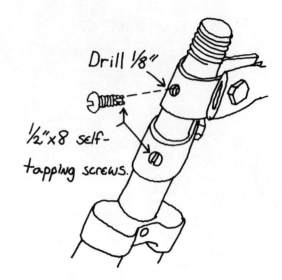

Drill 1/8"

1/2"x8 self-tapping screws.

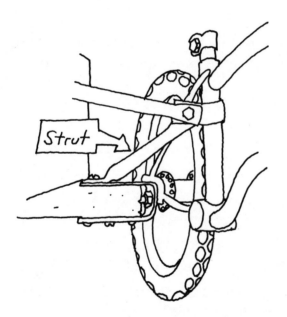

Strut

The more rigid a rig like this is, the better it'll work. If it flexes too much try running another conduit strut from the clamp on the seat stay to the two-by-four axle strut, and fasten it with a 1-1/2-inch #10 screw. This can be a short one attached to the strut next to the box, or it can run through the box and be attached at the far end.

8. "YOU'RE ON YOUR OWN" PROJECTS

Here's your chance to do some inventing yourself. This section is just ideas, and they haven't been tried out like the rest of the projects in this book, so you'll have to work out the details yourself. And you may end up with something quite different than you started out to build! But the ideas are basically sound, so if something strikes your fancy, go ahead. You're on Your Own!

WATER BIKE

With pontoons and a paddle wheel a bike can become a paddle boat. The floats could be made of almost anything—plywood, plastic sewer pipe, styrofoam blocks, or empty bleach bottles or five-gallon oil cans tied to a board, as long as they'll support the weight.

WILL IT FLOAT?

Find the load-carrying capacity of the float by figuring out the volume in cubic feet and multiplying that by 62 pounds—the weight of a cubic foot of water. If you're using oil cans or bleach bottles it's even easier, because "A pint's a pound the whole world round." So a gallon will float about eight pounds. You'll have to allow a good safety margin above this, at least 100 pounds above the weight of you and the device, or it will float—but just barely!

An easy way to build the paddle wheel would be by pop riveting blades cut from galvanized sheet metal directly onto an old back wheel. Make the blades as big as will fit through the frame.

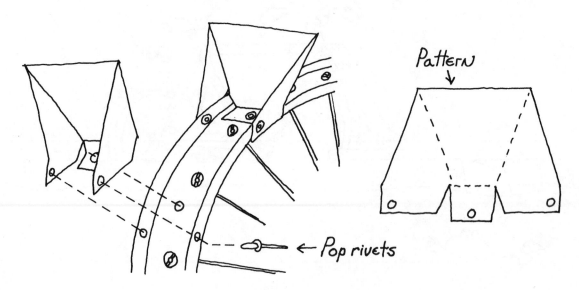

Pattern

← Pop rivets

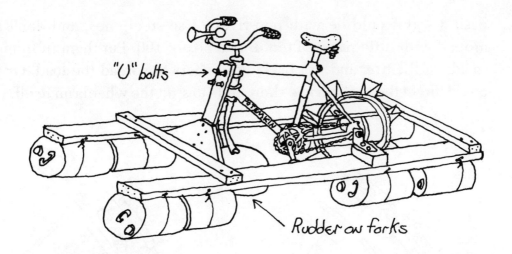

"U" bolts →

Rudder on forks

Here is one possible design using five-gallon cans for the floats, with the rudder attached to the bike forks.

ICE CYCLE

Don't count on using this on your neighborhood skating pond. It may cut up the ice pretty badly. But if you've got a lot of ice why not build two—they'd be wild to race! Stud the rear wheel for traction. The easiest way would be with pop rivets. Use steel ones, and don't fool around with little packs of ten. Buy a box of 100. Put them in from the inside of the tire, and use backing washers to spread the load. Or you could forget the tire and use short bolts to stud the wheel rim itself.

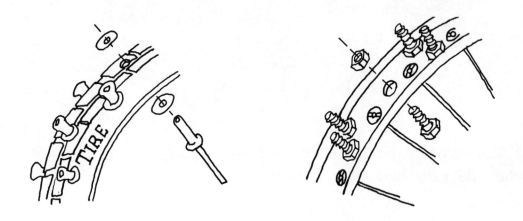

The trick is to find some way of steering, so the bike can lean into corners without slipping out from under itself. A crosspiece on the forks with old skate blades on it might work. Or how about some old training wheels from your junk box?

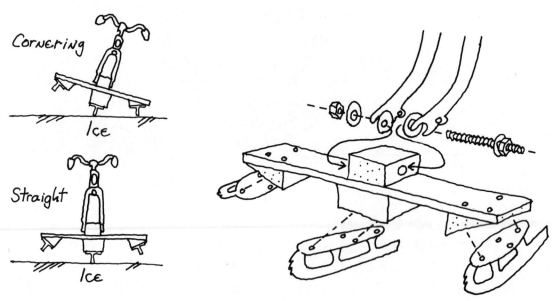

If you're really brave, try it with a single skate on the front forks.

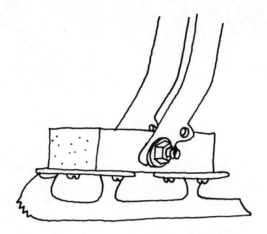

One last really strange idea. Try removing one crank and pedal completely, and put a toeclip and strap on the other. Use a single skate blade on the front forks, and ride it like a motorcycle flattracker, skidding around using one foot to hold up the bike, while you pedal with the other.

SUPER TANDEM

Why settle for just two riders? Why not three or four, or even six or seven? You'll need a heavily reinforced frame. Since bicycle brakes, forks and wheels won't handle the load try some from a small motorcycle. This won't be as expensive as it sounds because lots of smaller bikes end up in the junk pile when their motors give up. A bicycle chain isn't up to handling more than a couple of pedalers, so it would be a good idea to use the stronger motorcycle chain for the final drive between the last couple of cranks if you've got more than three or four riders. It'll take some fiddling with the gear ratios to get it right since motorbikes gear up where push bikes gear down.

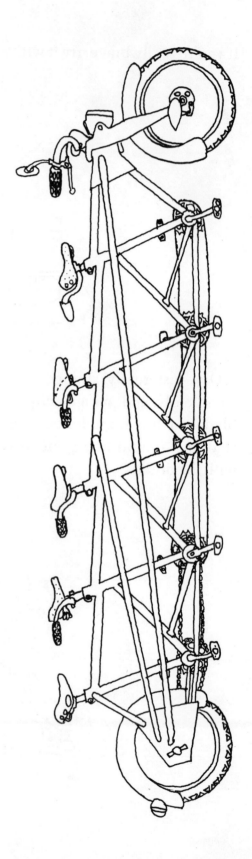

Use **EMT** thinwall electrical conduit tubing to reinforce the frame. The motorcycle forks could be welded complete with their head tube to the bike frame, and an oversized dropout cut from steel plate to adapt the back motorcycle wheel.

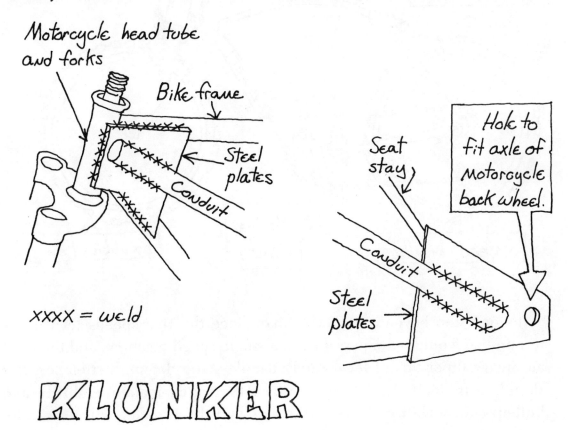

KLUNKER

Klunkers seem to have first sprung up in backwoods northern California, where people who had been using old clunker bikes for dirt riding kept improving their mounts with parts from other machines. They're used for cross-country woods riding and even hairy downhill racing on steep dirt fireroads. The Klunker combines a bit of everything: the indestructible frame from the American clunker, the gears from the dérailleur, lightweight and the knobby tires from the BMX bike. Somewhere in the future there will probably be ultra-light titanium Klunkers at 800 bucks a copy, but for now there's only one way to get one: Dig out your collection of old parts and build it yourself.

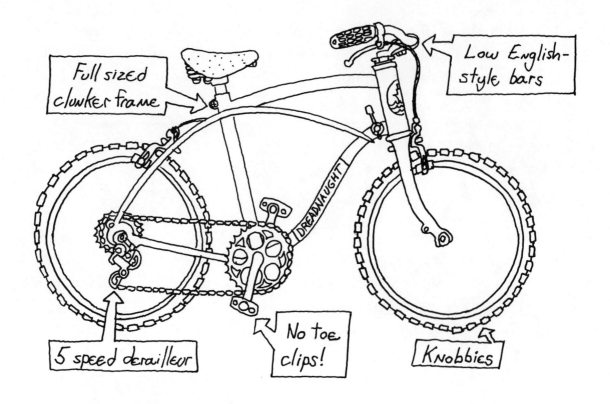

Full sized
clunker frame

Low English-
style bars

5 speed derailleur

No toe
clips!

Knobbies

It's one step beyond the BMX bike, since the five speeds let it cross terrain that would be impassable on a single-speed machine, and the front and rear caliper brakes let it safely handle steep downhill stretches. But there's a tradeoff. In return you lose the quick maneuverability and bulletproof reliability of the BMX bike, and the Klunker will need a lot more attention to keep it running. So it's really a bike for the more experienced rider.

You'll need to lace up a special back wheel using a balloon tire rim and a dérailleur hub, held together with heavy-duty spokes. Handlebars from an English three-speed work nicely as a compromise between high BMX bars and low drop bars.

Making Bikes Work

TOOLS

The following are the basic tools you'll need before you can build any of the things in this book. Most of them you should probably buy—even if they can be borrowed—if you like working with tools, because you'll be using them all the time.

Wrenches - Since bikes use so many oddball sizes, it would be good to have a couple of Crescent (adjustable) wrenches. A few open-end or combination wrenches in frequently used sizes, 7/16 inch, 1/2 inch, and 9/16 inch, for example, are handy but not essential.

Hammer   **File**   **Pliers**   **Hacksaw**

Screwdrivers - Since these should fit the slot in the screw fairly well, you really need three: a big one, a small one, and a Phillips (cross-slotted) head.

Punched steel bike wrenches - These cost a couple of bucks each at the bike store. Each one fits a lot of hard-to-fit foreign nut sizes, and they are thin enough to fit in places, like on a wheel-bearing cone, where a regular wrench won't fit.

Penetrating oil - This is the scavenger's best friend, a special oil for freeing rusted and frozen parts. Give the part a good dousing, let it sit for a few hours or overnight, and you'll save yourself a lot of trouble. Better yet, you won't have to mangle potentially usable parts while trying to get them off. Liquid Wrench brand is very good and available everywhere—buy a large can! It isn't for lubricating, though, so use something else on your chain.

Tire spoons - These are levers with blunt ends especially made for prying bicycle tires on and off their rims without puncturing the tubes. Get them from a bike shop.

Those are the absolutely essential tools. The following are either needed only for the harder projects, or are just good tools to know about, even if you can probably get by without them.

Vise grip (locking) pliers - These are big, mean pliers with hardened teeth and a powerful locking device. They are unbeatable for frozen or rounded nuts because they lock onto them very very tightly and dig in for a good grip. But be careful when using them on anything good. They are not gentle. You can also use them as a portable vise for holding small things while you saw or drill them. Buy only the genuine Vise Grip brand or the copies Sears sells, as there are some pretty terrible imitations around.

Electric drill - You'll need a drill frequently, and it's one of those tools you can probably borrow. But since you can get a pretty good one for around fifteen dollars, you might consider buying one. The plastic ones Rockwell makes are very cheap and almost indestructible. These go on sale a lot, so watch discount house ads. Get one with a 3/8-inch chuck (the chuck is the part that actually holds the drill bit).

You can also use your drill to wire brush or sand. If you do, BE SURE TO WEAR SOME KIND OF EYE PROTECTION. You can buy cheap goggles that work fine at any store that sells tools. This is very, very important. (There are some safety rules that you can ignore if you're very careful, but this is not one of them.)

A few tips on using a drill:

—Put a few drops of oil on the drill bit before drilling. It'll cut better and last longer. If the going is heavy, stop to let the drill bit cool off frequently.

—*Be sure your work is held down well when you're drilling.* The bit has a tendency to grab when it goes through. If the work is loosely held it can rip free and spin around, hurting you. If you don't have a vise try nailing the work down loosely to a larger scrap of wood. I like to hold the work on the ground with my feet. That way if it spins loose it'll just hit my shoes or ankles, which are considerably tougher than my hands (or eyes)! The wood underneath will also keep the drill from dulling itself on a cement floor or drilling into your workbench.

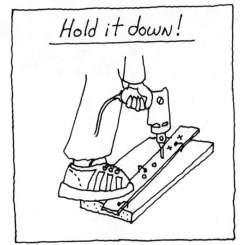

—Once you've figured out exactly where you want the hole, strike a nick in the metal with a center punch. This gives you a spot to start the drill in and keep it from "skating." You can buy a proper center punch at a hardware store, or improvise one (which will need resharpening alot!) by sharpening a big nail.

Drill bits - Get only those labeled *High Speed Steel* or HSS. This means they are made specially for use in drilling metal. Anything else is junk, and won't last long. HSS drills are more expensive, but you'll only need a couple of sizes for anything in this book.

Strap wrench - You can easily make this tool for undoing anything that won't fit your Crescent wrench out of a foot of pipe and 18 inches or so of nylon strap or an old belt. Use it by wrapping the strap around the object to be turned, in the direction it is to turn. Once it's all wrapped, pushing the handle will exert turning force on the object while tightening the strap's grip on it. The strap wrench is especially good on headset nuts and other large or odd-shaped parts because it'll fit anything and won't damage the finish.

Tapered reamer - This tool is a real favorite of mine and gets a lot of use. If you can't afford a complete set of drills it's the next best thing. Stick it into a hole and twist it back and forth, and it will make the hole bigger. It'll cost about five dollars from a good hardware store.

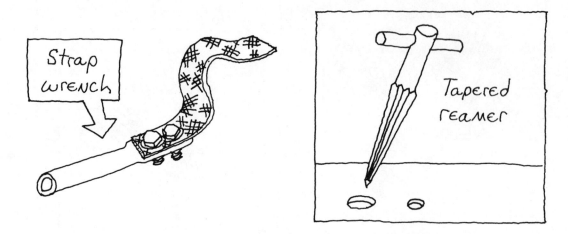

Wire brush - An oversized toothbrush with stiff steel bristles, it's great for removing rust, and the only way to get threading (like on a bolt) really clean.

Vise - A good vise is essential if you're going to be doing any heavy bending and comes in handy all the time for holding things to be drilled or hammered. Vices are very expensive, so check around and you can probably find one you can use occasionally.

BALL BEARINGS

If this section seems to pay a lot of attention to bearings, there is a good reason why. Ball bearings are the secret of the bicycle's amazing efficiency. Every last moving part of a bike moves on them and they eliminate friction and wasted energy. If they didn't, the bike would pedal as if it had two flat tires.

These bearings need regular attention if the bike is going to run its best, but they do their job so quietly that they usually are forgotten or horribly neglected. Most of the work in salvaging an old bike will be in taking apart, cleaning, greasing, and adjusting these bearings. It's fun work because you'll really be able to feel the difference when it's done!

The different bearings on the bike are each covered individually later on, but the basic procedure is the same for all of them.

TAKING THEM APART

While a few very new bikes use one-piece sealed bearings, almost all bikes use the old style where individual balls run between two races, usually a cup and cone, one of which can be screwed in or out to adjust the bearing or take it apart.

On some American bikes the balls will be held together in a retainer (sometimes called a cage), but otherwise they'll be loose and just waiting to fall out and get lost, so keep a container handy to catch them in and spread a large rag under where you're working to keep any that do fall from bouncing off and rolling away.

CLEANING

Once apart, clean the races and balls carefully in a can of kerosene or paint thinner. Don't use gasoline for cleaning. It works, but creates fumes that can easily explode. If you're dumb enough to insist on using gas, use only the very least necessary, and use it outside so the explosive fumes won't accumulate. And watch out for flames, cigarettes, heaters, etc., anything like that can touch it off.

If the balls are rusty, pitted, or you've lost a few, replace the whole set. They're cheap. Take an old one along when you go to buy new ones. They come in lots of sizes. You'll probably want to use the races no matter what shape they're in because they aren't so cheap. Polish them with a bit of fine steel wool until the bare metal shines.

GREASING

Bearings should be greased—not oiled. Oil isn't tough enough, and won't stay where you want it. All-purpose automobile grease works fine and you can usually bum enough for free to do the job. If you have to buy it, a tube of outboard motor or snowmobile grease, such as the Sta-Lube or Lubriplate brand, is especially good because it's extra resistant to water. Stick the balls onto the cup with a heavy layer of grease. Use a generous amount, completely covering them, and the grease will hold the balls in place while you put the bearings back together.

If you've lost a few balls or just aren't sure how many went where, keep in mind that the balls should be loosely spaced in the race. It is usually possible to squeeze in one more than there should be, but they will be packed in too tightly, making it impossible to get the adjustment right.

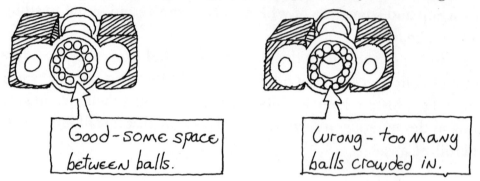

Good—some space between balls.

Wrong—too many balls crowded in.

ADJUSTING

Once the bearing is back together it must be adjusted by screwing one of the races in or out. A well-adjusted bearing has just enough clearance, or play, to turn freely but not enough to let it wiggle. To get this, tighten the adjusting cone or cap down while turning the bearing, until it starts to bind, or to turn with noticeable resistance, then back off a dab. This is something you'll have to acquire a feel for.

If it's impossible to get a bearing to adjust properly, or it seems to be right, then loosens or tightens itself, that's a sign that something is wrong. Take it apart and check that there aren't missing balls, or too many crammed in, or that you haven't mixed different sizes, or that something isn't crooked or crossthreaded (see Crossthreading, page 88).

Bottom Brackets and Cranksets

The bearings in the bottom bracket are very important to the efficiency of the bike, and are the most neglected of all. To check them remove the chain. If the pedals won't spin smoothly, quietly and absolutely freely, or if their axle can be wiggled up and down, they need attention.

Several different designs are used, and each comes apart differently. The most common type is the cotter pin crankset used on English and European bikes. To remove these, first drive the cotter pin out and remove the crank arms. Knock off the slotted lock ring and unscrew the bearing cup. Then withdraw the axle and the rest of the ball bearings, and unscrew the other bearing cup.

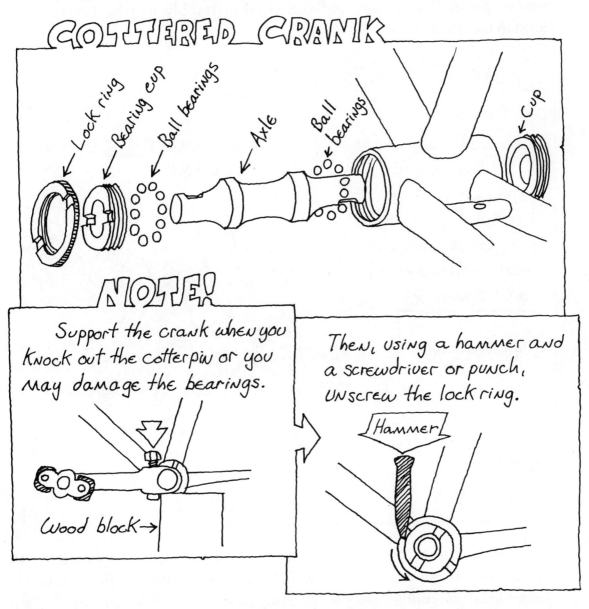

The Ashtabula or one-piece crankset, a different system, is used on some Schwinn models and other American bikes. This uses a one-piece crank, chainwheel and axle assembly. To disassemble, remove the pedal on the side opposite the chain wheel, then undo the large nut on the axle part of the crank. It'll probably be a left-handed thread, which unscrews clockwise, the opposite way from normal nuts. Remove the washer and dust cover, and the adjusting cone can be undone with the end of a screwdriver. Now remove the ball bearings, and the crank assembly can be twisted out through the bracket.

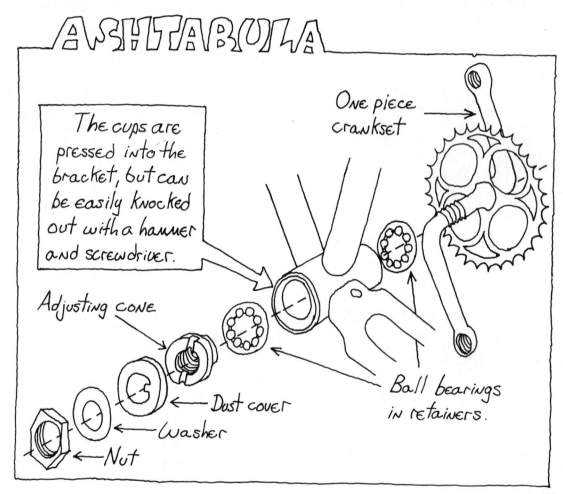

Be careful not to get the bearings in crooked when you put it back together, as this is easy to do. Check that everything is turning freely several times while tightening down the adjusting cone.

There is also a cotterless crankset used on good ten-speeds. If you find a bike with one of these you're in luck, because it's a good one. But servicing it needs special tools, so it's a job for your bike shop!

Once apart, all the different kinds of bottom bracket bearings, with the exception of the rare sealed-bearing kind, are treated the same. Clean them, replace bad or missing balls, then grease and reassemble, adjusting them carefully as you do.

Some brackets are equipped with an oil hole on top. Don't pay any attention to it—the proper stuff to use is grease, not oil. Treat it the same as one without an oil hole.

Pedals

Each pedal has two sets of bearings, one on each end. To get to them pry off or unscrew the dust cap, depending on how it's held on, and undo the locknut and adjusting cone. Then the pedal can be pulled off its spindle (spilling ball bearings all over the place).

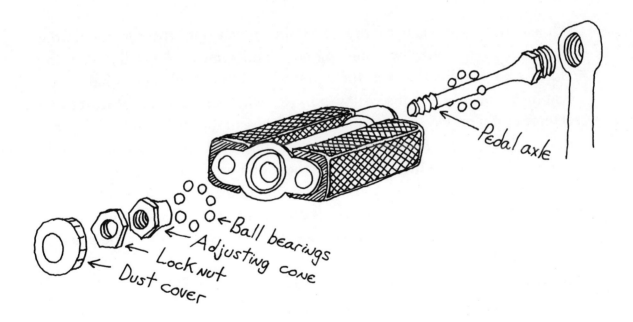

If you've taken the pedals off their cranks be careful when replacing them: left and right pedal spindles and cranks may be threaded in different directions. Check before forcing!

Wheel Hub Bearings

All front wheels, and rear wheels too on dérailleur bikes, use the same bearing setup shown here. Coaster brakes and three-speed hubs are a slightly different barrel of snakes and are covered elsewhere.

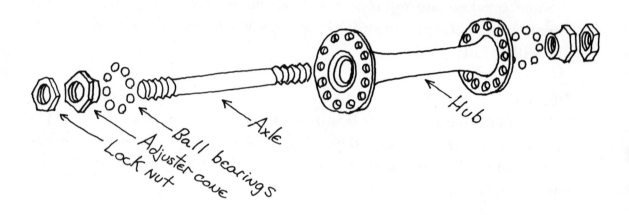

On each end of the axle there's a locknut and washer. Unscrew them from either side along with the adjusting cone and remove the balls. Now the axle can be withdrawn from the other side, along with cone, balls, and what-have-you. Some hubs will also have a dust cap over the bearings or a retainer on them. Pay special attention in reassembly that the bearings are adjusted just right. Any little looseness that will be barely noticeable anywhere else on the bike will really show up here, as the fifteen inches of wheel radius multiplies it. This wobble doesn't just make the bike unsteady—it wastes energy. A bike with wobbly wheels takes, in effect, a long cut wherever it goes, covering more distance to get to the same place!

Headsets

Nothing tricky here. These are the bearings the fork turns on. Two cups are pressed into the frame's head tube itself. The bottom cone is on the forks. Play is adjusted by loosening the lockring and screwing the top cup up or down. To dismantle them completely the handlebar stem must be removed first.

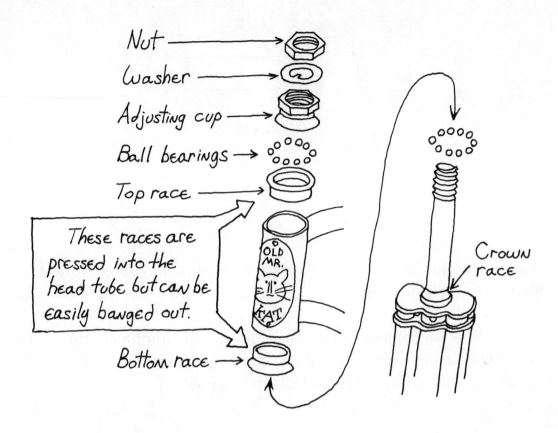

Nut

Washer

Adjusting cup

Ball bearings

Top race

These races are pressed into the head tube but can be easily banged out.

OLD MR. KAT

Bottom race

Crown race

OTHER PARTS

Frames

There are all kinds of different frames, some considerably stronger than others. It's good to be able to tell the difference, especially if you're building a tandem where the load will be much heavier than on a single seater.

Good frames will be lugged. Lugs are the metal fittings that join the individual tubes.

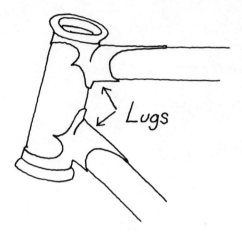

Some Schwinn models are exceptions to this and have very good unlugged frames. Other than that, lugless frames are used on the cheapest bikes and are not very strong.

Look where the dropout and the stays meet. On better frames the joint is neatly brazed and ground smooth; on the cheaper, more flimsy frames the stays are hammered flat where they join the dropout.

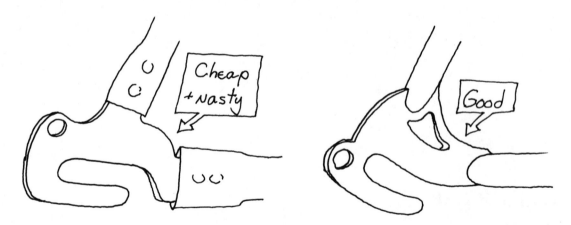

The quality of the welds is another giveaway. On decent frames the joints are usually brazed at lower temperatures, then ground smooth. The cheap ones are electric welded without any grinding or touching up after.

But beggars can't be choosers, so don't turn down a cheap frame. Use it until something better comes along but don't spend a lot of time or money fixing it up.

Handlebar Gooseneck (or Stem)

These come in a lot of different sizes, depending on where the bike was made. They are held in by a wedged jam nut that expands the stem of the gooseneck down inside the fork stem. To remove, loosen the bolt 1/4 inch or so and bang it down with a piece of wood. If you must use a hammer, put a piece of wood on the bolt head before you strike so you don't damage the bolt. Once the jam nut is driven down, the stem can be pulled up and out.

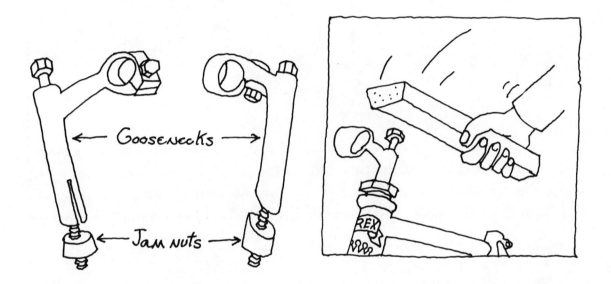

On some types you'll need to bang the jam nut lightly into the stem then take up the slack in the bolt before replacing the gooseneck, or the jam nut will turn with the bolt when you try to tighten it.

Seat Posts

These also come in a lot of different sizes. Be careful always to leave at least 2 to 3 inches of seat post in the frame. If you need more height get a longer seat post. Actually, if you need more height at the seat than the stock post provides, you really need a bigger frame. But you're not likely to find one of them in the trash, and seat posts are cheap.

Brakes

A bike without good brakes is not safe to ride. Foot dragging may seem to work most of the time but is useless when you need it most—on a steep hill, or when a car cuts in on you without warning. Even if the rest of the bike is old and worn out, keep the brakes working like new!

Many older bikes use back pedal hub brakes. These don't always work so well when they're old. Flushing them out with Liquid Wrench, then oiling as for a three-speed hub may get them working, but the easiest fix is to throw a caliper hand brake on the front wheel. The front brake has much more stopping power than the rear, because in a fast stop most of the weight is on the front tire, which gives it better grip on the road.

Weak caliper brakes can usually be fixed with new blocks. Get these from a bike shop since some of them work much better than others, and at a bike shop they'll know which. Be sure to get the blocks on the right way or they'll fly off the first time you use the brakes.

The biggest problem with caliper brakes is that they don't stay centered with the wheel, and one of the pads drags as you ride. The only cure for this is trial-and-error adjustment until you get it just right.

Check that the calipers both move freely on the shaft. Then loosen the nut on the other end of the shaft that holds the brakes to the bike, and move the brake assembly in the opposite direction from the side that has been rubbing. Retighten the nut and check the setting by applying the brakes hard several times. Remember that it's the spring and spring anchor that really determine the setting, and they must be tightened down for the brakes to stay adjusted. It's possible to push the calipers themselves into a false adjustment that will disappear the first time you use the brakes, which is why you should recheck the setting frequently by jamming the brakes on and off with the lever while you are adjusting them.

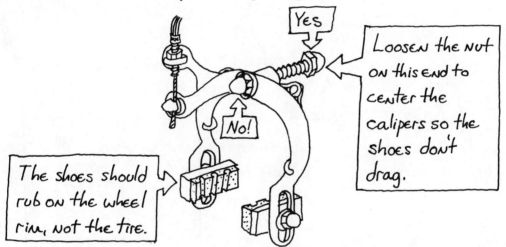

Since each side of the brakes won't necessarily move exactly the same distance when you apply the brakes, it may be that when your brakes are adjusted right they won't look centered, but will hit the rim at the same time and not rub when they're not on.

Gears

Most bikes have either three-speed hubs or dérailleur gears. With either, proper adjustment makes all the difference in the world. Three-speed hubs must be kept oiled inside. A "teaspoon full of oil each month" is the recommended amount. Don't use sewing machine or Three-in-One oil—it's too thin and may evaporate. Use proper bicycle oil or, better yet, buy a quart of 20W nondetergent auto oil and an oilcan, and give it a squirt every month.

To adjust, unscrew the chain from the cable and check that the indicator rod on the end of the chain is screwed in, finger tight, all the way. Then put the shift lever in high, and reconnect the cable to the chain. Tighten the cable until there is just a little slack left in it and the chain and rod have not begun to be pulled out. That should be the right setting. Double check by putting the shifter in second gear (N) and looking in the hole on the hub nut. The indicator rod's end should be just level with the end of the axle. On

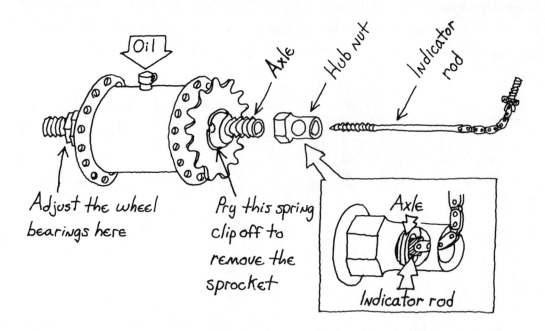

older, more worn-out hubs some additional trial and error may be necessary to get the adjustment just right.

Some newer three-speeds use a lever instead of a chain. On these put the control lever in N and adjust so the letter N is visible in the little hole in the hub nut.

If there's not enough cable length to get a proper adjustment on any three-speed move the cable fixing clip on the frame tube back or forth to lengthen or shorten the free cable.

Three-speed hubs have bearings, just like any other hub, which need occasional adjustment. This is done as on a normal hub by loosening the locknut and adjusting the cone.

Dérailleurs look a lot scarier than they are. They're all a bit different, so if you can find specific instructions for yours you're that much ahead. Basically, though, they all are adjusted the same way. Somewhere on all of them you'll find two little screws that limit the dérailleur's movement outward and inward. Set these so the cage can travel in each direction far enough to easily slip the chain onto the outermost sprockets, but not far enough to jump it clear off. The cable should be adjusted first to allow the dérailleur its full range of movement—when it's in its loosest position there should be just a tiny bit of slack. Adjusting will be much easier if you can rig up some way to get the bike off the ground so you can hand crank the pedals while watching the gears working.

Don't overlook the chain when you're troubleshooting a balky dérailleur (see Chains, page 85). The chain is an important part of the ten-speed system, and the best dérailleur will shift poorly with a cheap or worn out chain.

Check the chain tension too. The chain should still be tight when it's on the smallest sprockets, front and rear. Adjust if necessary by moving the wheel forward or backward, or if that's not possible, by removing links.

The front dérailleur is much simpler, but the adjustment is basically the same as the rear; allowing enough travel to jump the chain cleanly but not throw it off. Also it can be moved up or down on the frame to give the correct clearance (about 1/8 inch) between the cage and the larger chainwheel. Oil the dérailleurs when you oil the chain, putting a drop of oil on all the pivot points and wiping off the excess so it won't pick up dirt.

Both kinds of gears are too complicated to repair much beyond lubricating and adjusting. Very little ever goes wrong on a three-speed and when it does, another used one is usually easy to find. Dérailleurs, on the other hand, especially cheap ones, get out of whack in mysterious and aggravating ways. Here the best solution may be to throw it out and get a new one. Why am I going against everything I've been saying in this book to tell you this? Simple. A bad dérailleur makes for really unpleasant riding. And the better low-priced Japanese dérailleurs are probably the biggest bargain in cycling today. An especially good value is the Suntour V series. The VGT or VXGT is a perfect replacement for lousy original-equipment gears and can be had for about twelve dollars from a bike store or eight dollars from a mail-order house.

Kickstands

If you've got a kickstand lying around and want to use it, go ahead. But don't waste your money on one. They add weight and don't work well anyhow. A slight breeze can blow the bike over, and the merest shove will upset it. Lean the bike up against something or lie it on its side (it'll end up there often enough even with a kickstand). Leave it chain side up. This will keep the chain cleaner and protect the gear-shifting linkages or dérailleur.

Wheels

Loose spokes should be tightened and missing ones replaced. This can be done if there aren't too many bad ones, without throwing the whole wheel off if you tighten the spokes up very cautiously making sure not to overtighten the new ones. Check that none of the ends stick through on the inside after replacing spokes. If they do, file them down flush with the nipple or you'll soon have a punctured tire!

If a wheel is out of line have a bike store look it over. If the rim isn't bent they can probably true it for four or five dollars. But if the rim is gone start looking for another wheel.

Tubes and Tires

Bike tires have tubes inside to hold the air. A puncture usually won't hurt the tire but just the tube and that can be easily fixed with a fifty-cent tire patch kit from a hardware or bike store. Follow the directions that come with it.

For some reason a lot of people put a new tube and tire on whenever they have a flat. So you can often find usable tubes and tires around if you know how to patch a few leaks.

Probably more bike tubes are punctured when being changed than while on the road. Prying the tire off the rim with a screwdriver is a sure way to put a hole in the tube. Try to learn to put tires on with your bare hands. That way you can't puncture anything. If you work the tire onto the rim a bit at a time it isn't too difficult. If you can't manage this, get some tire spoons.

Schwinn, incidentally, uses some tires and rims of their own special design. These do not interchange with other makes, so watch out for mix-ups. Rims and tires for Schwinns will usually be so labeled.

Chains

A chain should be kept clean and lightly oiled. Old chains, no matter how bad they look, can usually be revived by soaking them in kerosene or penetrating oil for a few days, then scrubbing them clean and oiling them. But a worn chain wastes power, making pedaling harder, so if a chain is really worn, and you're riding the bike a lot, replace it. If you just need it for some nutball device you're cobbling up, use an old chain, by all means.

To check the chain for wear, lie a section down on a flat surface. Hold it with both hands about 5 inches apart and push the links together; then pull them apart. If there is noticeable "play" the chain is worn out. Also try moving one end back and forth to the sides while holding the other end rigid. There should be no more than 1 inch of play on the moving end. This is especially critical if the chain is being used with dérailleur gears.

When you need a new chain, avoid like the plague the three-dollar ones department stores sell, especially if it's for a ten-speed. A good chain will improve the shifting of any dérailleur, and a bike store is the place to find one.

Chains can be lengthened by joining two together with a spare master link (this is a special link that comes apart so the chain can be taken off). Shortening a chain is a lot harder. The easiest way is with a tool, called a chain breaker, made especially for the job. A bike store can do it for you in a minute or so or you can buy one for three dollars or so. If you're stuck without these, the simplest way is to pick the link you want broken and file off the peened over stud, then hammer it through and out with a nail set or nail.

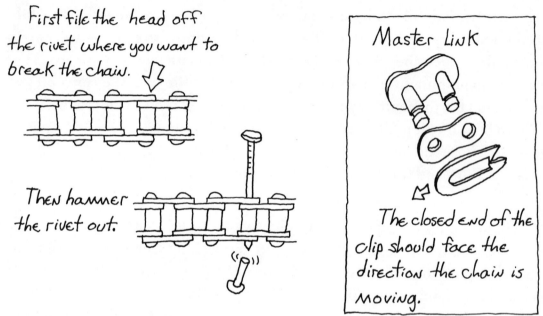

First file the head off the rivet where you want to break the chain.

Then hammer the rivet out.

Master Link

The closed end of the clip should face the direction the chain is moving.

Dérailleur chains don't use a regular master link since the clip could foul on the gears. For these chains you'll need a special link, one that is pressed together with pliers, from the bike shop.

Whether you're starting with a new chain or a salvaged old one, remember the only cause of chain wear (unless you ride thousands of miles a year) is poor lubrication—keep it oiled!

Gear Ratios

A bike's gear ratio determines how easy the bike is to pedal. To figure it out divide the number of teeth on the chainwheel by the number of teeth on the rear sprocket. This will give you a ratio that tells how many times your legs must push the cranks around to turn the rear wheel around once. For example, a bike with a 44-tooth chainwheel and an 18-tooth rear sprocket has a ratio of about 2.4 to 1. To lower the gearing so the bike is easier to pedal you need a chainwheel with less teeth, or a rear sprocket with more teeth for a ratio of, for example, 2.2 to 1. To make the gearing higher, so the bike will pedal harder but go faster, do the opposite, for a ratio of say 2.6 to 1.

Most three-speeds and coaster brake hubs have a removable sprocket held on by a spring clip. Pry it off with a screwdriver to switch sprockets and change the gearing. Or the front chainwheel can be changed as for the BMX bike (pages 11–12). On a ten-speed the rear wheel sprocket cluster can be replaced, but you'll need special tools.

Threads

Threads are not your high-fashion cycling outfit, but the twisty spiral grooves on nuts, bolts and other parts that hold the bike together. These come in different sizes and thread counts (the number of grooves cut per inch) depending on what country the bike was made in.

In general, British, Japanese and lightweight American bikes use one thread pattern, European bikes another, and heavier American bikes yet another. But there are plenty of variations even in these groups.

It's usually no use trying to force mismatched threads together because it'll just ruin both parts, although there are a few oddball combinations that will work sometimes. If you're not sure, try it, but gently. This really only matters when the threads are cut into the part itself, like the frame or the cranks and pedals, so it shouldn't cause you too much trouble.

Threads are easily damaged, so handle them with care. If they don't undo easily try soaking them with Liquid Wrench (see Tools, page 67) overnight before using force, and clean them with a wire brush before putting them back together.

There are several ways to salvage damaged threads. The proper way is to recut them with a die or tap, special tools for cutting threads. These are expensive and hard to find in offbeat bicycle sizes, so you'll have to take the part to a bike shop and let them do it. This is a last resort though, because they'll want money. Often, you can get a bolt through from the other side of a female (nut-type, inner) thread, as in the case of pedal holes in the end of cranks, which are usually damaged on the outer side and run in and out to smooth out the damaged threads. A small triangular file can be used carefully to recut damaged parts of a male (bolt-type, outside) thread.

CROSS THREADING

Cross-threading is when the inside and outside threads are started crooked in relation to each other.

These threads seem to be screwing into each other for a turn or so but get harder and harder to turn, and finally jam. This is because one set of threads is trying to recut the other set crooked. Needless to say, the further you force it, the less chance you'll have of ever getting it in straight. Back it off and try again.

As a general rule, something should go together more easily than it came apart. If it doesn't, make sure everything is O.K. before forcing. The wider something is, the greater the chance of cross-threading. The bottom bracket cups and the headset nut are good examples of parts easy to cross-thread. The more banged up the threads are, the greater the chance, too.

Outside threads that have been hammered on are usually spread at the end and won't fit even though the threads may look o.k. File down the end, taking care to leave a good lead-in thread to start the nut.

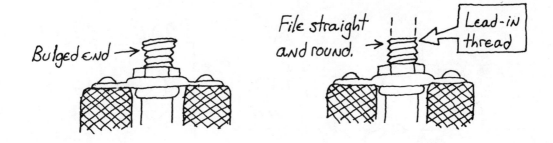

Your best defense is to remember when you're taking the bike apart that you'll be putting it back together again, so treat all threads with respect.

Nuts and Bolts

If you need a nut or bolt to fit some specific thread on the bike, you'll have to get it from a bike shop, because the odds are it'll be a foreign thread your hardware store has never heard of. Otherwise, just use the nearest American size, which will be a lot easier to find.

Nuts and bolts aren't all created equal, but come in different grades according to how strong they are. The little marks on the head of each bolt identify the different grades. Hardware store bolts are usually the lowest grades, or not marked at all. Don't worry—for most applications they'll be plenty strong. Sometimes, though, you'll need a really strong bolt, either because the size you can fit in a certain spot is limited and you need all the strength you can get or because you tried a hardware store bolt and it broke. The easiest place to find them is an auto parts store—not a tires and appliance type store, but a real auto parts shop selling engine parts that has a parts counter where they wait on you. Bring an old bolt along so you'll get the size right and ask for grade five.

A good collection of nuts and bolts, and screws in all sizes, or a "miracle box" as old-time mechanics call it, is hard to get along without. An easy way to accumulate one is to always strip any machine your family or any of the neighbors are throwing out. Washing machines, old car motors and lawn mowers are usually loaded with usable bits.

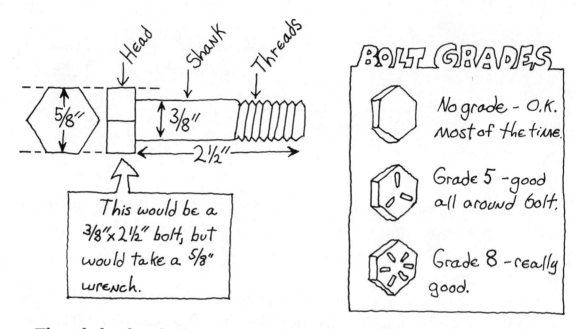

This would be a 3/8" x 2½" bolt, but would take a 5/8" wrench.

BOLT GRADES

No grade - O.K. most of the time.

Grade 5 - good all around bolt.

Grade 8 - really good.

Threaded rods, which you can get from the hardware store, are handy too. These are lengths of steel rod threaded like a bolt over their entire length. Hacksawed to size they're just the thing for making up on the spot that odd length bolt you need but don't have. The catch is that they aren't made of very good steel and aren't nearly as strong as a good bolt. Put a few nuts on the rod before hacksawing it off. Then if you mangle the threads you can screw the nuts back and forth to straighten the threading. If you forget to do this it can be very hard to get a nut started on the cut end.

On most machines lock washers are used with nuts and bolts. These are special washers that keep the nut and bolts from loosening. I haven't used them in this book because bikes don't vibrate, so things coming loose aren't a problem, but it's good to know what they are in case you ever need them.

Bolt and screw sizes are given by the width followed by the length, so if directions call for a 3/8" x 2 1/2" bolt it will be a bolt 3/8" across and 2 1/2 inches long. That is too say, 3/8" on the shank, not the head. Since the head is larger it would take a 5/8" wrench. Confused?

Screws and bolts smaller than 1/4" come in number sizes, sometimes followed by the thread size, then the length, such as 8-20 x 3" which would be a size 8 bolt with 20 threads to the inch and three inches long. You'll catch on to these sizes from using them, so don't be afraid to ask to see some different sizes at the hardware store if they're not out in the open.

Since there are different thread counts, usually a choice of coarse and fine thread, even in American sizes, what it all boils down to is that you'd better take a sample of what you need whenever possible, or buy nuts and bolts together so they'll match. Anyway, most hardware stores only stock coarse thread in most sizes, so it's not quite as complicated as it sounds.

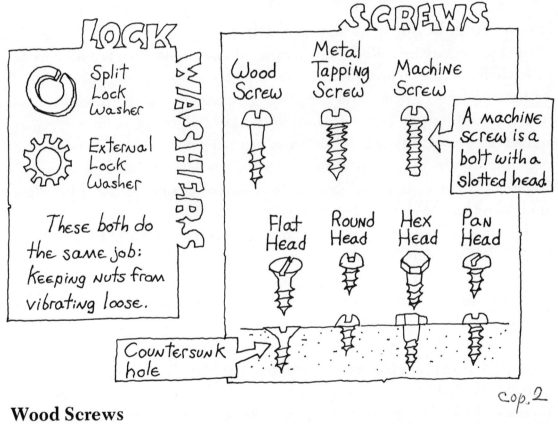

Wood Screws

Wood screws come with several different head styles. Use round heads when the head will stick up and flat heads when they'll be sunk into the wood. It's a good idea to drill a hole a bit smaller than the wood screw

91

before screwing it in. It'll go in easier and be less likely to split the wood. Try rubbing a bit of soap on the threads to make them go in easier.

Another useful screw is the self-tapping metal screw. These have hardened threads so they, like the name says, tap their own threads as they go in. To use these, drill a hole a little undersize and force the screw. If it won't go try a slightly larger hole. A tapered reamer (page 69) will come in handy here.

Making Bikes Better

Hammering, Bending and Improvising

All of these may be called for, and how you go about them has a lot to do with whether you end up with a nice-looking recycled bike or a junker.

First of all never hammer a threaded part directly on the threads. That makes instant junk. When you absolutely have to hammer a threaded part protect the threads first. Sometimes you can put a nut on it and hammer the nut. Other times you can put a piece of wood on the part and hammer on it. Professional mechanics use brass or lead hammers that, being softer than steel, won't hurt.

Chrome is also very sensitive to hammering and should also be protected by a block of wood under the hammer.

The same sort of problem turns up in prying and bending. Often an attempt to bend a tube will just flatten a section, either where it's being bent or where your pry bar or piece of pipe is braced. Once again, the right way is to distribute the force evenly, using a block of wood, a rag, or anything to spread out the force and protect the part.

Most bikes fall into one of several groups. There are the old balloon-tired American bikes, the English three-speeds, and the latest fad, ten-speed racing bikes. In general, parts can be switched easily among different nationalities and makes of bikes in any one group with one important possible exception mentioned earlier: threaded parts. Parts can also be

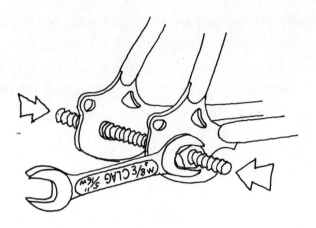

switched between groups, but it'll take some ingenuity and wider to fit a different wheel. One neat way to do this is to use a piece of threaded rod in place of the axle with nuts and washers on the inside to spread a frame, or on the outside to squeeze it. By turning the nuts the bending can be done in a careful and controlled way, and only just as much as is necessary. (This is hard to do by flailing at the frame with a hammer.) Bending weakens, though, so don't overdo it.

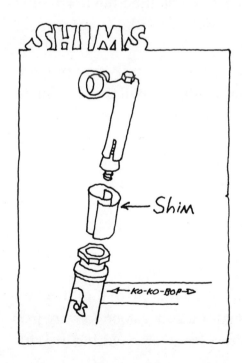

SHIMS

←— Shim

←—KO-KO-BOP—→

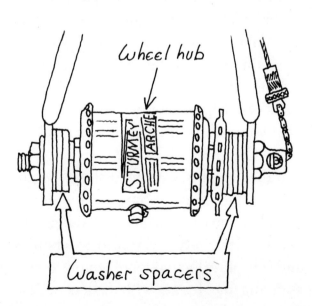

Wheel hub

STURMEY ARCHE

Washer spacers

A narrower wheel can be put in a wider frame by stacking washers on each side of the axle as spacers. Stacks of washers as spacers are useful in lots of other places, too, because the washers can be added or substituted one at a time to adjust the fit, or in the case of a wheel, moved from one side to the other to line up the chain properly.

Shims—strips cut from a tin can—may be wrapped around a handlebar to make it a snug fit in a larger gooseneck, or around the gooseneck stem to fit it into a wider fork stem.

The possibilities are endless. Each case will be different, calling for different solutions. But with enough work, imagination and fiddling almost anything can be made to fit anything else.

Paint

New paint can turn your pile of recycled parts into a real bike. For a slick professional finish, and a wide choice of colors, try the expensive little spray cans of auto touchup paints found in the auto department of any discount store. Since this paint is made to match the original paints on cars, you can get it in almost any color imaginable from metallic blue to firemist pink. Swinn bike paint, sold by Swinn bike shops, is excellent, and since it comes in bigger cans, is cheaper to use.

How well the paint job turns out depends on how carefully you prepare the frame. While you might get away with just sanding down the old finish, use paint remover (be sure to wear gloves) and steel wool to remove all the old paint if you want to do a really good job. Spray the frame with several coats of cheap primer paint before using the good stuff. Use fine sandpaper or steel wool to smooth down mistakes and rough up the surface between coats of paint.

If the old paint is in good shape but dull from age you can bring it back by using some auto rubbing compound—a sort of toothpaste for paint—or a self-cleaning car wax on a rag, along with a lot of elbow grease.

Consider safety and visibility when you refinish a bike. Use bright colors and lots of reflective tape. If you're not trying for a super good job, try just spraying the frame with reflective Day-Glow paint or covering it with reflective tape. This will be flashy, easy to see day or night, and make it easy to spot your bike if it's stolen.

Chrome

Good bicycle chrome is hard to kill. An abrasive chrome polish will usually bring it back to life, no matter how rusted and pitted it looks. The stuff you want comes in a tube, not a bottle. Simichrome, sold in motorcycle and bike shops, or Duro chrome polish sold in hardware stores (which is a lot cheaper) are both excellent.

If the chrome is badly rusted, steel-wool it all off, then rub silver paint over the chrome with a rag. The paint will stick where the rust was but can be polished off the chrome, camouflaging the bad spots.

All these things—steel wool, polish, paint, and what not—add up fast if you're buying them. But a bicycle doesn't take much of any one of them, so look around and you can probably borrow some from someone you know and save your money for things you absolutely have to buy.

Welding

The place to get welding done is a shop that specializes in it. These are listed in the yellow pages. For bike work the smaller shops specializing in odd jobs and repairs are best. Tacking gussets on a BMX frame or welding a tandem together should only take a few minutes and cost under five dollars. If no one can recommend a shop to you, try calling a few and explaining what you want. If the shop you call doesn't do small jobs like yours ask them if they know one that does. Then take the work to the shop that seems most agreeable about doing such a small job and doesn't have an unreasonable minimum charge (some shops have a minimum, like fifteen dollars, or the rate for one hour's work, which they charge for all smaller jobs).

You may have a neighbor with a welding torch in his garage or a mechanic at a local gas station who'll attempt anything. Be careful! Bicycle tubing is very thin and a strong weld is important. An inexperienced welder can easily goof the job and ruin the frame. If you do let a friend or any nonprofessional welder do it, dig up a junk frame they can practice on. If you have any doubts take the job to a welding shop.

Buying Steel

Often these projects will call for flat stock strap or angle iron (which is also steel—the name "iron" just stuck). Hardware stores carry a small selection, but usually nothing bigger than 1/8 inch thick, and way overpriced. Looking up Steel in the yellow pages will usually just give you the numbers of places selling it by the ton! What you need is something in between. This will probably be a welding or steel fabrication shop that stocks steel for their own use and will sell it in small quantities. How can you find a place like this? Start by asking at your hardware store. If they can't send you to the right place look up Steel Fabricators in the yellow pages. Call a few of them and explain what you want, and you should find it.

Often these places charge one price for the steel stock—usually by the pound—plus an additional cutting charge if you buy less than a standard length. Don't be afraid to ask—before they've cut your order—how they charge. It may be cheaper to buy a bigger piece and hacksaw it yourself, especially because you'll have some left over for another time. Or they may have a scrap from another order that's close enough to what you need, and will save you from paying the cutting charge.

Odds and Ends

Bargaining

Anytime you're looking to buy something secondhand, know what it would cost new. You can find this by looking in the Sears or Wards catalogues if they list the item; if not, call a store selling what you need and ask. You shouldn't ever pay more than half the new price for anything used, and rarely even that much. Knowing the new price helps you to bargain.

Three dollars? But brand new it's only three-fifty—how about taking a dollar for it?" you can say. You'll probably get it. Always ask if whatever you're buying is returnable if, for some reason, it's not usable. You might not get any promise of getting your money back, but you should be able to exchange it for something else.

"Look, Kid, Do you really have money to buy that or are you just wasting my time?"

If the stuff is being sold "as is," and no returns are allowed, which is usually the case at a junk store, then the price should be considerably lower because you're taking a risk. This is a good bargaining point.

I'm not even sure it'll fit," you can say, or "Well, the rim and spokes look o.k., but there's no way to tell if the gears are."
Usually the owner will make a counter offer. "Well, would you pay two dollars for it? But at two dollars if it's no good I don't want to hear about it. I'm losing money on it!" And you've got it.

Mail Order

If you're in the market for any expensive new parts—dérailleurs, wheels, or saddles, for example, you should know that a lot of the better stuff is available at considerable discount from mail-order supply houses, most of whom advertise in *Bicycling!* magazine. If you're trying to upgrade a ten-speed, they could save you a lot, or make it possible to use top-quality parts for the same price as second-rate stuff bought locally. For example, a

Suntour GTV dérailleur that costs thirteen dollars and fifteen cents in stores, cost me six-fifty plus seventy-five cents shipping from a mail-order house.

Disadvantages are that some mail-order houses are sometimes back-ordered and cannot ship your merchandise until they get it in—several months sometimes! Returning things is troublesome and costly because postage must be paid both ways.

If this doesn't scare you off be sure when you order to specify how long you're willing to wait if they can't ship immediately and whether you'll accept a substitute item. If the stuff never comes, write a nasty letter to the company. If that doesn't work call the post office and file a complaint. There are very strict laws now governing mail-order sales.

Buying from a mail-order house recommended by friends who have had good luck with it cuts down the risk considerably. Also, on a larger order especially, have it sent UPS (United Parcel Service) COD—if possible. This costs a dollar more, but you won't have to part with your money until the goods are in your hands. If they never come you've lost nothing but time.

In conclusion, if you know exactly what you want and want it as cheaply as possible, and don't mind waiting a couple of weeks (possibly longer), mail order is for you. But if you need a part right away or aren't sure exactly what you need, go to a bike shop.

Bikecology, P.O. Box 1880, Santa Monica, California 90460, and Bike Warehouse, Box 290, New Middletown, Ohio 44442, are two of the bigger ones that I've had good luck with. Bikecology especially puts out a great catalog.

Selling Bikes

If you're a success at accumulating old bikes and parts it might occur to you to build up a bike or two to sell. The secret to making this pay is substituting your own labor for money and not spending a cent more than you have to. Old chrome parts brought back to life by lots of polishing (or wrinkle black paint if it's hopeless), a repainted frame, a seat shined up with shoe polish, and well-greased and adjusted mechanicals should be enough to get a good price. Any new parts you use will cut into your profit. There are some exceptions. New tires, if needed, should pay their way, and some new smaller parts, like brake blocks and new handgrips always impress the potential buyer.

Once the bike is finished check out some bike stores to find out what similar bikes are selling for. Don't fool yourself, but be honest in your comparison. A ten-year-old machine with a repainted frame is not in the same league as a two-year-old bike with original paint, even if they are both English three-speeds. Once you've got a good idea of what it's worth at the shop set your price at least ten dollars lower. If there's a bike shop you're on good terms with you can just ask them what they think you should ask for it. But it's easier to lower a price than raise it, so keep your opening price a bit on the high side.

If you can't always find a customer among your friends, then advertise. If you live near a college campus put ads up on bulletin boards there. Coin-operated laundries and supermarkets usually have notice boards where you can leave ads. Most areas have throwaway newspapers or classified ad magazines offering free classifieds (sometimes you have to buy a copy to get the coupon for sending in the ad). Lots of people read these. For some reason, the cheaper an ad is the better it works. Free classifieds always seem to work better than the ones you pay for.

One thing bad about advertising is that it can attract professional bargain hunters who can be very pushy. Their kind will tell you your bike is junk, lie about the price of a new one to make yours look overpriced, and act generally indignant that you, a kid, won't gratefully take anything they offer. In their eyes these are all fair bargaining techniques. Your defense is to know just what the bike is really worth. If you've done your homework, you will. Besides, you'll know that if they didn't think it was worth pretty close to what you're asking they wouldn't hang around bargaining!

One last caution: When you sell someone else a bike, you are responsible for it. Someone has paid good money for it and is entitled to a trouble-free machine in return. This is why the bike store can get more than you for the same bike. They stand behind it with their reputation. So shortcuts and worn-out parts that you can live with on your own bike won't do here. But if you're willing to spend the time it'll be well worth it. Enough scavenged parts to build two or three three-speeds along with some paint, grease (elbow and regular), and polish could be turned into the price of a good new ten-speed—or a really great used ten-speed—those classified ads can work both ways!